The Amazing Adventures of SUPERPONY!

Janet Rising

Matador
9 Priory Business Park,
Wistow Road, Kibworth Beauchamp,
Leicestershire. LE8 0RX
Tel: 0116 279 2299
Email: books@troubador.co.uk
Web: www.troubador.co.uk/matador
Twitter: @matadorbooks

ISBN 978 1800461 406

British Library Cataloguing in Publication Data.
A catalogue record for this book is available from the British Library.

Printed and bound in Great Britain by 4edge Limited
Typeset in 11pt Minion Pro by Troubador Publishing Ltd, Leicester, UK

Matador is an imprint of Troubador Publishing Ltd

For Helena

Chapter One

As SHE GAZED OUT of the car window, the seat belt digging into her shoulder, Hannah couldn't stop fidgeting. Every turn of the car's wheels took her closer to her dream. She didn't dare speak because she'd already been told off a dozen times for blabbing on and on – so much so that her parents, their ears ringing, had threatened to change their minds. She was, they had told her, driving them mad!

Hannah wriggled about with her lips pressed tightly together, her mind racing. If she didn't calm down her dream might not come true, and if that happened she would simply die, she thought. Or burst. Or burst... into flames! If she burst into flames she might burn the horse dealer's stables down. And if she burst into flames and burned the horse dealer's stables down then she might not...

"This must be it." Her dad interrupted her galloping thoughts as he turned the car into a neat stable yard with a number of horses and ponies looking over their stable doors. Soon, Hannah told herself silently, one of these beautiful creatures – the most perfect one – would be hers, and her new life as Hannah, the-person-who-could-do-something-well, would start! Before she had even got out of the car she had spotted a perfect dappled grey. And there was a shining bay with a white blaze, a palomino like Florin and a quizzical piebald. Hannah wanted them all. How would she ever make up her mind and choose just one? Which one would prove to be the most perfect pony of all?

For Hannah, it was vital that her parents bought her the perfect pony because up until now she'd been pretty rubbish at practically everything she'd attempted, and she was convinced that a perfect pony could change her life – change Hannah herself, in fact. At school she was below average at English; she came somewhere between middle and bottom in science and she was nearer to the bottom than the middle in maths. Hannah's parents had always told her that one day she would find something she enjoyed doing and then, they'd assured her, she'd be really good at it. Hannah had clung desperately to that thought.

The trouble was Hannah had got fed up with trying to discover what she might be good at. It certainly wasn't sport. Hannah dreaded PE lessons. Running anywhere seemed to take ages; her high jump wasn't; her long jump was too short. She was never able to throw a ball into a net or hit one with a racket or a bat. No-one at school picked her for their teams. Instead, she became a member by default, holding her breath, her face turning puce, desperate to hear her name called as all her classmates were selected before her.

"Oh no, we've got *Hopeless Hannah*," her unfeeling team mates would whine when Hannah was the only one left to choose and therefore relegated to their side. "We'll never win now!" It was as though Hannah couldn't hear them, or had no feelings to hurt. It wasn't unknown for the last choosing team captain to offer Hannah to the opposing team as a handicap, which is about as insulting as you can get.

But now Hannah had put all the insults behind her because she was getting *a pony*, and it had to be the *perfect* pony.

Hannah was certain that getting the perfect pony was going to change her life because a perfect pony would change *her*.

Completely.

She'd never been more sure of anything.

Ever.

Chapter Two

THE DEALER WOMAN WITH ponies to sell (how could she bear to sell any of them, wondered Hannah) shook hands with her mum and dad, and there was a lot of grown-up talk exchanged as Hannah gazed around, breathing in the warm, sweet smell of horses. She felt energised by it, as though she worked on batteries that recharged with every equine breath. The dealer woman was very glamorous with very, *very* blonde hair held back in a ponytail by a large, bejewelled clip. She wore very long, very shiny black boots, and she was squeezed into the tightest jumper and pair of jodhpurs Hannah had ever seen, which hugged her curves as if she'd been poured into them. The dealer woman seemed to have a lot of curves. She seemed to go in and out more than most women. She was, thought Hannah, searching her brain for a word she'd learned in geography the other week, very *undulating*. Her teacher had used the word to describe how land went up and down in hills and valleys, but it seemed to be the perfect word to describe how the dealer woman's figure worked, even though the surface in this case was vertical rather than horizontal. Hannah's dad seemed *very* taken with her. I bet she sells a lot of horses to men who are taken with her, thought Hannah, for loads and loads and *loads* of money.

It had been several months since Hannah had begun riding lessons with her friend Jessica – her *best* friend Jessica she had been then – and they had both started in the same riding class. As soon as she sat in a saddle Hannah knew that riding was going to be the thing she was good at because she *loved* it. She vowed she would never, *ever*, give up riding, full stop. Hannah had given up so many hobbies and pastimes before.

Like archery. Hannah's arrows had sailed past the target and stuck into the ground instead. Sometimes, they had sailed past someone else's target way down the line and, occasionally, they had somehow headed off in the opposite direction from the targets altogether, as though terrified of them. Hannah's arrows had certainly terrified the rest of the archery class.

No, archery hadn't been the thing Hannah was destined to be good at.

And then there had been gymnastics. It looked so easy on the television, and Hannah had given it her best shot, but she didn't seem to have any spring or sense of rhythm. And really, how was anyone supposed to be able to do any exercises on the mat when there were always so many other people on it, too? No wonder there had been collisions. Even so, being described by the tight-lipped coach as a liability had seemed harsh. Hannah had decided that gymnastics hadn't shone its light on her, either.

She'd given up ballet (all those leg positions designed to trip oneself up – very dangerous), and violin lessons (why stand everyone so close together if a violin bow can do that sort of damage?), and drama club (because it's very easy to fall off a stage when there are bright lights shining in your eyes, *actually*), but she wasn't giving up riding, no way! When Hannah had her lessons with Mrs Evans at Lavender Riding School she felt like a different person, a person who could *do* something – she'd even got the hang of rising to the trot before Jessica had. It had never happened to her before, the feeling of being better than absolutely hopeless. Plus, the ponies were just so gorgeous, with velvety-soft muzzles and manes which tickled her face when she hugged them. Hannah was determined to be a rider. A good rider. She just *had* to be.

Of course, Hannah and Jessica had been stomach-wrenchingly jealous of the girls who had their own ponies.

"I wish I was Fi, her pony Florin is just beautiful," Jessica had sighed. Florin was an eye-catching palomino pony with a coat the colour of newly-minted gold which contrasted with his snowy-white mane and tail. Fiona, known as Fi, was a year older than Hannah and Jessica, and she and Florin had won loads and loads of rosettes at shows – judges were mesmerised by the vision of the golden pony with his flaxen-haired rider as they cantered around the show ring.

Also successful was Ellie, with her strawberry roan mare Strawberry Pop, and the pair were always winning or being placed in show jumping classes. Ellie's chestnut pony tail, which bobbed under her hat, was a perfect match for her pony's as they tackled fence after fence, concentration showing on the rider's face as she cut corners and asked Strawberry Pop for more effort, riding determinedly through the finish flags.

Hannah and Jessica dreamed of getting their own ponies like Florin and Strawberry Pop, and of becoming best friends with Fi and Ellie. The trouble was, Fi and Ellie lived on Planet Pony Owner, and Hannah and Jessica were in another atmosphere altogether. Fi and Ellie weren't even aware that Hannah and Jessica existed because the privately-owned ponies were stabled on a separate livery yard, away from the hustle and bustle of Lavender Riding School's ponies, pupils, parents and lessons.

While Fi and Ellie groomed and rode their gorgeous ponies, Hannah and Jessica invented their own imaginary dream ponies. Jessica's was a dappled grey called Cloud who was good at dressage and jumping, and Hannah invented a black pony with a white star called Major, who was a three-day eventer and carried her to victory at all the big events. In Hannah's imagination, Major would allow no-one but his talented mistress to ride him, and her favourite dream was one where she beat everyone at the local show, her parents beside themselves with pride, Fi and Ellie congratulating her with huge smiles and asking for top tips to improve their own performances.

To her excitement, the dealer brought out the dappled grey pony Hannah had seen from the car and the groom, a girl of about eighteen, rode the pony around the field for them all to watch and see how well mannered and well schooled it was, and how perfect it was for someone like Hannah to ride and own. The groom was nothing like as glamorous as the dealer woman, but rather tubby and grubby, with brown hair crammed under her riding hat. She sniffed a lot. The grey looked like a rocking horse, with a pretty head and flowing mane and tail, and Hannah fell in love there and then. *This* was her perfect pony, she thought, for *sure*. Hannah imagined how her status would soar at the riding school if her parents bought this dappled grey pony, and how it would totally transform her and how she was perceived. She would become a perfect match for the beautiful grey mare – serene, elegant – it was meant to be! Hannah fastened her hat and body protector – she couldn't wait to get up into the saddle.

The dappled grey was nothing like the riding school ponies Hannah was used to riding. It floated beneath her, responding willingly to her aids. Most of the riding school ponies argued and dared their riders to make them do things in a jolly, trying-to-teach-them sort of way. This pony was used to obeying its rider's every command. *Would you like me to trot? Canter? Jump? Turn left? Turn right? Just ask!* The pony begged to be instructed. They popped over a jump and returned to the field gate where

Hannah leapt out of the saddle and ran to the grey's head to give it a pat. But the dappled grey mare put back her ears and scowled at her. It was anything but friendly, reserving its well mannered demeanour for work under the saddle. *Don't push it*, the pony seemed to say, eyes glaring, ears flat back against its neck.

"She's a lovely pony," the dealer woman assured Hannah's parents, seemingly oblivious to the less-than-lovely faces the mare was pulling. "Your daughter will go far on her, I'm sure."

Hannah gazed wide-eyed at her mother to indicate that she had no desire to go for even a short way on this unfriendly pony. To her relief Hannah heard her mum say, "I think Hannah would like to try some more ponies before we make up our minds."

Things had started to go wrong when Jessica got her own pony. Not a grey like the imaginary Cloud, but a chunky brown-and-white pony with a black mane and tail, called Roxy. With her black plaits and round cheeks Jessica seemed a perfect fit for Roxy, just as Fi matched Florin, and Ellie complemented Strawberry Pop.

"Of course, you can ride her, too," Jessica had told Hannah. "I don't mind sharing her with you. After all, you're my best friend." And Hannah had been very excited and couldn't wait for Roxy to arrive. But when she did, Jessica became an inhabitant of Planet Pony Owner, and Fi and Ellie suddenly became aware of Hannah's best friend, upgrading her to their own. And because she had Roxy, Jessica's riding got better and better and she was soon elevated from Hannah's beginner class to one for better riders. And naturally Jessica spent more time at the stables than Hannah, who just had her riding lesson and then went home. It didn't seem at all fair but Hannah couldn't do anything about it. Jessica owned her own pony and she was too busy to hang around with a beginner who rode the school ponies and wasn't able to ride whenever she liked. Of course, Jessica never *actually* said that to Hannah, but Hannah knew it to be true all the same.

Despite these disappointments, Hannah refused to give up riding. After all, she had decided that riding was what she was going to be good at, with or without Jessica (who Hannah started referring to herself in private as *The Traitor Jessica*). If I were The Queen, thought Hannah, I'd have Jessica thrown into the Tower of London to reflect on how she's changed. And then I'd confiscate Roxy and it would serve *The Traitor Jessica* right.

But of course, Hannah wasn't The Queen so that didn't happen. And deep down in her heart Hannah knew that even if she were The Queen (which wasn't on the cards because queens are pretty good at stuff and Hannah was sure queens were born, not made), she probably wouldn't have Jessica imprisoned, no matter how much her friend hurt her. Besides, Hannah was almost certain that queens didn't do that sort of thing any more.

Chapter Three

THE SNIFFY GROOM LED out the palomino. It was a little bigger than the dappled grey and its golden coat gleamed in the sun like a flickering flame. It was like Florin only even more beautiful – a fairy pony. Hannah gasped. She had been mistaken. *This*, she thought, is the pony I love, not the grey. *This* is the perfect pony.

Hannah and her parents watched the palomino canter around the field with the groom on board. Even under Sniffy, as Hannah had named her in her head, it was an impressive display. If I have this pony, thought Hannah, everyone at the riding school will be wildly jealous. Deciding that this would be no bad thing she eagerly mounted and adjusted her stirrups. The palomino behaved as well as the grey, and Hannah was certain that this glamorous pony was the one for her. It was a no-brainer!

She heard her dad laughing heartily at a remark from the dealer woman. I'd better decide on a pony quick, thought Hannah, before Mum gets fed up and decides we have to go, or Dad pays too much for a pony I don't want! Her dad was laughing the way he did at Christmas and at family weddings when he'd had a few glasses of wine. He didn't make very good decisions then, either, according to her mum. Dismounting, she winked encouragingly at her mum and went to the pony's head for a chat.

But the palomino was no friendlier than the grey – it stared into the distance, ignoring Hannah completely. *You are not worth even acknowledging*, it seemed to say, its nose in the air as though Hannah smelt of something nasty. Hannah changed her mind and pulled a face at her mum, who asked the dealer woman what else she had, in the same way she asked the woman on the deli counter in the supermarket whether she might suggest something different from their usual cheese.

Hannah could tell by the dealer woman's face that she was miffed. Hannah could tell from her mum's face that she didn't care. She was getting fed-up with Hannah's dad hanging on every word issued from the dealer woman's very red lips.

The dealer woman thinks I'm fussy, thought Hannah. And mad. She shows me two beautiful ponies and I'm not satisfied. But she has lots of ponies and I can only have one. She doesn't understand how right it has to be. It has to be the perfect pony!

Because riding was the one thing Hannah refused to give up, her parents had got very excited and decided that her new-found enthusiasm needed nurturing. They hardly dared hope that this was the activity at which their hopeless daughter might possibly shine. After all, hadn't Hannah's riding teacher, Mrs Evans, hinted to them that Hannah's riding skills held potential for future Olympic glory? The possibility that Mrs Evans might drop hints of this nature about most of her pupils in order for their parents to book a few more lessons somehow escaped them. They grasped desperately at the straw, however implausible, and readily agreed that their daughter would progress much quicker, and would be certain of future equestrian glory, with a pony of her own. In addition the pony could, Mrs Evans assured them, be accommodated at Lavender Riding School for a modest monthly sum. Hannah's father had disagreed about the modesty of the cost, but he was persuaded by the female side of the family to agree to the plan anyway.

Hannah had wanted to scream and shout and dance and sing whenever she'd thought about getting a pony of her own. In the weeks between being told she could have a pony and actually going to the dealer's yard Hannah, overcome with excitement in school lessons, had sometimes asked to go to the toilet, even though she hadn't needed to. She had half-ran, half-walked along the corridor, locking herself in a cubicle and punching the air, mouthing a silent, *Yes! Yes! Yes!* before taking a deep breath and returning to class to see what else she could do in a bottom-to-middling sort of way. She had performed even worse at her school subjects than usual because she had day dreamed about getting her pony when she should have been concentrating. She couldn't wait for her riding to improve in leaps and bounds, just as Jessica's had when Roxy had come into her life. She would soon be someone who was good at something, they'd see!

I'll show everyone that I'm not stupid or dim or *hopeless*, Hannah thought. My pony will turn me from *Hopeless Hannah* to *Clever Hannah*. I'm going to be a different person with my perfect pony to help me. This is the start of the new me! Hannah had promised herself this at least seven times a day, and probably as many as sixteen times a day at weekends.

Hannah tried the bay mare with a white blaze. She was nice enough but she didn't seem perfect either, although Hannah couldn't put her finger on exactly why. Then she had a go on the piebald, and that wasn't any better. It was very disappointing. Hannah could feel her heart sinking – she had been certain she would find her dream pony at this yard, on this day. What was wrong with her? What was she looking for? Would she find it? Did it even exist?

Leaving Sniffy saddling yet another pony, and her parents talking with the dealer woman (more pathetic chuckles from her dad), Hannah explored the stables. She spoke with a big black horse, exchanged a few words and whinnies with an iron grey, patted another, bigger bay cob and then, just as she was turning to go back to try the almost ready, rather chubby dun pony which was the latest on the list, heard a whinny which she couldn't ignore. Following the sound she spotted a stable tucked around the corner. At first it looked empty, but Hannah popped her head over the door and got a surprise.

A chestnut pony lifted his head and rushed to the door. *Hello!* he seemed to cry, nuzzling Hannah's hands. *Got any sweets?* The pony nudged her pockets and left half-chewed hay all over her sleeve. Hannah laughed. This pony wasn't stand-offish or stuck-up. She stroked his neck (he had a dirty-grey mane which was all different lengths and stuck out in all directions, as though he'd slept badly on it); she patted his nose (it was snotty and he didn't mind wiping it on Hannah); and she whispered in his ear (the pony made nickering noises and talked back to her).

Hannah was smitten.

"Can I try the chestnut pony round the back?" she asked the dealer woman.

The dealer woman stared at her in astonishment, one eye twitching slightly, her lips parted. Hannah thought she saw her exchange a glance with Sniffy, who raised her eyebrows. Snapping her very red lips shut the dealer woman scratched her ear and her eyes darted left and right for second. Then she broke into an ever-so-sincere smile, and when she spoke her voice was like honey – extra sweet and smooth.

"Well that particular pony has only just come in with a shipment from Ireland… but, er, he comes highly recommended," she crooned. "Of course we'd be delighted to show him to you. I don't know why I didn't think of him before, he's *perfect* for you!"

It sounded promising – but then Hannah remembered the dealer woman had said that about all the other ponies she'd tried that morning.

The pony was tacked up for the groom to ride. Out of the stable Hannah could see that his chestnut coat was patchy and his tail matched his dirty-grey mane, the colour of pencil lead, all spiky and facing every-which-way. Under his bushy forelock she could see a small, smudgy white star, and the colour of his ginger legs faded over his knees in a half-hearted manner, draining to a wishy-washy pale, not-quite-white colour where they met his grey hooves.

The pony danced about while the groom tacked him up – he seemed very excited at being included in the party. Glancing at her mother, Hannah could see she was comparing the chestnut with all the other ponies, and he wasn't coming out of it well. Well, you didn't have to be a genius to see that he wasn't as glamorous as the dappled grey or the palomino, thought Hannah.

As the groom rode him in the field the chestnut snatched up his knees and snorted at the jumps. He jumped them well, however, shaking his head when he landed as though surprised by his achievement. He looked as though he was really enjoying himself. He looked – Hannah struggled to find the right word – he looked *happy!* Hannah didn't know why she was so drawn to this pony but she couldn't deny that she was. It was as though he had been waiting for her, and all the other ponies were just there to make her realise that the chestnut was the one for her.

When Hannah sat in the saddle she felt an instant connection. The pony turned his head and snorted. *Oh, it's you. Well let's go,* he seemed to say, and they walked, trotted and cantered around, finishing with a couple of small jumps. When she went to his head after dismounting, the pony nuzzled her and nickered softly, in complete contrast to the other ponies. Hannah felt a connection and images of a beautiful and perfect pony drifted away. This pony was THE ONE!

"What's his name?" she asked, stroking his nose.

"Er, well he hasn't got one," said the dealer woman. "To be perfectly honest with you Mr and Mrs Pearson, he's just off the boat yesterday, but if you want him I can let you have him on a week's trial. That way, if you change your mind, one of the other ponies will suit, I'm sure."

"That's very reasonable of you," said Hannah's dad, giving the dealer woman the benefit of a wide smile.

Hannah looked at her mum. Her mum knew what that look meant.

"Are you sure you wouldn't rather have the dappled grey, darling?" her mum asked, bewildered. "She's such a *beautiful* pony."

Hannah shook her head and held on tightly to the chestnut's reins. She could feel his breath on her arm. It felt warm. It tickled. It blew the tiny hairs on her arm the wrong way.

"The yellowish one is an impressive pony," said her dad. He didn't much like the idea of buying a pony 'just off the boat'. "That yellow one looks very classy – you'll win rosettes with that one, I'm sure." The palomino pony was more his idea of a mount which would help his daughter shine at her chosen sport. Even to his inexperienced eyes the chestnut pony seemed cheap and nasty against the quality of the palomino. And it wasn't as though it were bargain basement, either – the dealer woman was asking almost as much money for the scruffy chestnut as she was for the palomino. Why did Hannah have to be so keen on this pony, for goodness sake?

Hannah felt a moment of panic. Would her parents refuse to buy the chestnut pony? She had to have him, she just *had* to. She couldn't explain the ache she felt in her heart, the wanting which had overtaken her thoughts. Before she had seen him Hannah was certain she wanted the dappled grey, the palomino, the bay or the piebald, a pony to be envied by everyone. But now, holding his reins, her head was filled only with thoughts of this funny, friendly, chestnut pony.

Hannah realised she could no longer feel the warmth on her arm. Could the pony be holding his breath – just as Hannah was holding hers? He wanted to go home with her and be her pony, she just knew it. He wanted to be picked, he longed to be included.

He's just like me, waiting for his name to be called out to join the team, thought Hannah. She couldn't leave him there, it was impossible. It would be… Hannah struggled to find the right word… it would be *cruel!*

"This pony is the one," she said, firmly. Images of dappled greys and palominos, of rosettes, of fast and beautiful ponies, of making everyone at the riding school jealous faded before her eyes. She wanted a pony who was going to be her best friend; a pony who was *happy*; a pony who was *fun*. She wanted the chestnut pony, just off the boat.

And that's how Hannah came to own the chestnut pony with the spiky mane and high knee action who nudged her pockets for sweets. And thinking about it later Hannah wasn't sure whether she had chosen the pony, or he had chosen her.

Chapter Four

O N THE DAY HANNAH'S chestnut pony was due to arrive at Lavender Riding School it seemed that everyone was there to have a good old nosey. The night before, Hannah had had dreams about riding her pony in the show ring against Florin (and winning), of competing against Strawberry Pop in a jump-off (and winning) and going neck-and-neck against Roxy in a gymkhana race (and winning). Hannah had woken up exhausted. But now, the dealer woman was letting down the ramp on her horsebox and a shrill whinny rang through the air. Her pony was here!

The crowd gathered around. A new pony was always news. Hannah remembered the excitement when Roxy had arrived: the tri-coloured pony had walked daintily down the ramp and stood solidly in the yard, allowing everyone to pat and fuss her, and Jessica had looked as though she might burst with pride. Hannah had been pea-green with envy on that day, and was looking forward to bursting with pride on this one.

The dealer woman disappeared into the horsebox and soon reappeared at the top of the ramp with the chestnut pony on the end of a rope. Hannah held her breath. Everyone was there watching: Fi and Ellie, Jessica, Joshua who owned Rambo the iron grey cob, a number of pupils and their parents, the riding school grooms and Mrs Evans, her instructor and owner of the riding school. Her audience!

He's here, thought Hannah, breathless with excitement.

He certainly was. Clattering half-way down the ramp the chestnut pony stopped, snorted and then took a giant leap to miss the bottom half of the ramp altogether, and landed in the yard, pulling the dealer woman behind him like a balloon on a string. Holding his head high like a giraffe, his mane wobbled about in more directions than you could count as he looked around, his nostrils flaring.

I am here! his whole demeanour seemed to announce, with great importance.

Whenever there was a new pony at the riding school, everyone got excited and couldn't wait to stroke the newcomer and ask questions. Hannah's chestnut pony was greeted with stunned silence. Hannah felt a niggle of doubt in her stomach. Her pony looked so comical now he was standing in front of everyone. Why didn't they say something? Where were all the *ohhs* and *ahhs* that always greeted new ponies? Everyone was strangely silent. Jaws were dropped. Eyes were widened. The niggle of doubt turned into a pang when Hannah heard someone giggle. It reached the gigantic proportions of a churn when she heard a snigger.

The chestnut pony didn't seem to notice. Dragging the dealer woman over to Hannah he dropped his muzzle into her hand. *There you are!* he seemed to say. Hannah was so touched that he recognised her, she forgot about the reaction he was causing.

"Er, what's going on with all that mane?" asked Jessica. Hannah ran her hand through it – it went north, south, east and west, as if it couldn't make up its mind where it was headed. Hannah's stomach-churning returned as her thoughts drifted back to the dappled grey and the palomino. There would have been *oohs* and *ahhhs* galore if either of those ponies were here with her now.

I can always take him back, she thought desperately. He's on a week's trial. This made her feel better. If it didn't work out with the chestnut pony then she could have one of the others, one that everyone was sure to admire. Why had she thought the chestnut pony was a good idea? She felt something like panic rising in her. Anyway, she thought, he's a pony and he's here now.

She patted her pony's neck and led him to his new stable on the livery yard, next to Roxy, where he promptly dug up his bed and rolled, throwing bedding around the floor and walls. When he got to his feet again, wood chippings clung to his mane and coat. He looked like a forgotten toy with its stuffing coming out. Not seeming to care he took a long, very noisy drink from his water bucket, dribbling water all over the floor before pulling at his hay net with greedy tugs.

"What's he like to ride?" asked Jessica. Everyone else had wandered off, exchanging eye-rolling glances and stifling giggles.

"Oh, he's lovely," Hannah replied, glad to have something positive to say.

"Perhaps you can ride him later and we'll watch," suggested Jessica, in a rather obvious effort to be kind.

"Mmmm," Hannah sort of agreed. She didn't feel keen for anyone to watch her ride now they seemed so unenthusiastic about her new pony.

"What are you going to call him?" Jessica asked.

"I don't know. I might not call him anything until I'm sure I'm going to keep him," Hannah replied. Now she had actually admitted she might not keep the chestnut pony she felt a bit better. She wasn't committed, she reminded herself. Nothing was cast in stone.

"Oh, can you swap him for something better... er, um, I mean something *else* then?" asked Jessica, a bit too eagerly.

"Oh yes," Hannah was surprised to hear herself say quite casually. "I shall see how he works out."

They gazed over the stable door at the chestnut pony. He had found some carrots Hannah had put in his manger as a welcome home present and was busy chomping on them. *Wow! Carrots!* he seemed to say. It appeared to Hannah that he wasn't used to getting treats and the thought made her uncomfortable.

"We'd better let him settle in," she said. Her pony (*for now*, she reminded herself) pushed his head between them to look out, dropping bits of carrot on to the yard as he did so.

Jessica went to find Fi and Ellie, and Hannah sat on a hay bale in the yard opposite her pony's stable, watching him. He dashed from his haynet to the door, shaking his head up and down and looking around him, then nickered to Hannah when he saw her. Hannah felt a pang of guilt. He liked her, this pony. Could she really swap him for another? She couldn't bring herself to use the word *better*, to describe the other ponies on offer, even though that was definitely where her mind was heading, probably because Jessica had said it – before she had corrected herself.

She decided to focus on something else to take her mind off her guilt. She had to think of a name for him. How about Conker? But no, the pony was nowhere near the colour of a conker. What colour was he? It was difficult for Hannah to put her finger on it exactly. He was chestnut, yes, but a rather dull, patchy kind of chestnut. It wasn't the sort of fiery red chestnut you often see and admire in horses – more a dirty brown. But, thought Hannah, I can't call him Chestnut, it was far too corny. Brownie was far too plain. What about a boy's name like Simon, or Henry, or William? They were all good names for ponies. But none of them seemed to fit. They seemed too, well, regal somehow. This pony was no king, he was more like a king's jester. Hannah sighed. Perhaps naming him wasn't a good idea, not if he wasn't going to stay.

Joshua came past on Rambo on his way out for a ride. An iron grey cob, Rambo's chunky neck was shown off by his hogged mane – clipped off completely by Mrs Evans every few weeks. He put Hannah in mind of a sort of equine Staffordshire bull terrier, and he always marched along like he was going to some battle which had to be won before the day was out. *Purposeful*, was how Rambo moved. Hannah's pony crammed against his stable door to sniff noses, but Joshua turned Rambo away.

"What sort of pony is he, exactly?" he asked Hannah.

Joshua had never spoken to her before – she had just been one of the riding school pupils and ignored. Being the only boy on a yard full of girls made Joshua very popular. Fi and Ellie were always trying to get Joshua's attention but he had always been well out of Hannah's league. Now she was a pony owner and her status had instantly shifted, something which wasn't lost on Hannah. She felt quite important – even though he was being rude about her pony.

What sort of question is *that*, exactly, Hannah wanted to ask. She longed to reply, *Oh, he's a Mark II Cyber pony*, or *Can't you tell, he's the last pony from the lost herd of Atlantis!* But she didn't.

"Well, he's from Ireland, just off the boat," she replied. She thought this made her sound quite knowledgeable.

"They didn't want him!" she heard someone say. It was Fi, giggling with Ellie as they strolled past, arm-in-arm, on their way to the tack room. Hannah stuck her nose in the air and pretended she hadn't heard them.

"He should be hogged, like Rambo," said Joshua. "That spiky mane of his is awesome – and not in a good way – it's all over the place. But of course," he added, "his neck's too scrawny for a hogged mane to look good." And he nudged the thick-necked, perfectly hogged Rambo towards the indoor school. "See ya, Spiky!" he added over his shoulder.

Mmmmm, it *is* spiky, thought Hannah. But she didn't want to hog her pony's mane. She decided she would train it to lie flat by pulling it over to one side of his neck and leaving it in plaits for days and days. That would sort it. Joshua wouldn't be able to say it was spiky when it was all trained and under control.

If the pony stayed, of course, she reminded herself.

Chapter Five

THAT AFTERNOON, HANNAH SADDLED her pony for her first ride. Her fingers trembled with excitement as she tightened the girth, and she held her breath as she mounted him in the school. After all, he was still her pony, and riding him was rather a thrill. True, getting there had been a bit of an ordeal... the pony had tripped coming out of the stable and had trodden on one of Hannah's toes. Then he had scratched his neck on the stable door and hooked his bridle over the bolt. As he had pulled back, one of the reins had snapped and Hannah had had to borrow a spare one from Jessica. And it hadn't stopped there because as she led her pony into the school he sidestepped, catching his saddle on the door, putting a nasty scrape in the leather.

"You're accident-prone, Spike!" Hannah told him crossly, the nickname prompted by Joshua's remark popping into her head without thinking. The pony looked anything but crestfallen by the accusation, but nudged her cheerfully instead. *Never mind* he seemed to say. He really was a very happy pony, Hannah thought. Nothing seemed to faze him.

Glancing up at the gallery, where people could sit and watch their nearest and dearest on their riding lessons, Hannah spied Fi, Ellie and Jessica – they weren't about to miss this opportunity for anything. Fi had one of the stable cats on her lap and she could see Ellie munching crisps. Ellie was always stuffing her face full of crisps – you could often hear the rustling of a crisp bag long before Ellie came into view. It was a wonder she didn't need a Shire horse to carry her, instead of little Strawberry Pop, Hannah always thought. But despite almost constant munching, Ellie remained as skinny as a rake.

The trio looked quite bored, and Fi and Ellie managed to look superior at the same time, which was quite clever of them, Hannah thought. She knew they were only pretending to be bored. They were there to watch her ride her strange, new pony, she was certain.

"Some people could learn a thing or two about attitude from you, Spike," she muttered under her breath as she swung into the saddle and found her offside stirrup.

Hannah rode around the school and her new pony (for now, Hannah reminded herself) did everything she asked of him. They walked, trotted, cantered and tried some 20 metre circles. The pony stopped when Hannah asked him to, and started again at her request. They even did some passable serpentines. He was a bit bouncy, and he did give the letters around the school a second – sometimes third – look, causing Hannah to lose a stirrup, but overall Hannah felt safe. A glance at the gallery showed that their audience seemed to be more interested in the cat than her new pony. Phew!

What's not to like, Hannah thought to herself. The pony was well behaved and eager to please, she felt confident and happy riding him, and he seemed to be enjoying himself, too. But deep down Hannah knew exactly what was bothering her – it was everyone's reaction to her new pony. She had seen Mrs Evans' look of surprise when her pony had leapt off the ramp. She remembered how Jessica had stared blankly at her chestnut pony, struggling to understand why Hannah had chosen this equine clown over other, surely more impressive, ponies. And there was Joshua. Even Joshua, who had never spoken to her before, had something rude to say about her new pony.

"I don't have to keep him," Hannah whispered to herself. "He's only on a week's trial. I can always have the dappled grey or palomino if I change my mind." But as she said it the pony stopped and turned his head to look back at her with his big, brown eyes. How could a pony look so, well, *disappointed?* Hannah shook her head, she was imagining it. But she felt guilty, too, as she remembered how she had found the pony round the back at the dealer's yard, in a stable out of sight. And then another thought occurred to her with a jolt, and she slid out of the saddle in horror.

"I don't think you were just off the boat," she whispered in the pony's chestnut ear. "I think you'd been at that dealer's yard for ages and ages, and nobody wanted you."

The pony pushed his muzzle into her stomach and lowered his eyelashes. Hannah knew she was right. She had never been more certain of anything. Here was a pony nobody wanted. How could she send him back when he so desperately wanted to be loved? He wanted his own human as much as she wanted her own pony.

Hannah knew that dealers sold ponies to make money and the question loomed that if she didn't keep the chestnut pony and nobody else wanted him, then what would happen to him? What happened to ponies nobody wanted? Hannah knew that unwanted ponies went to the sales, and at the sales the ponies nobody wanted were bought by the meat men. How could she, Hannah, commit this happy (but clumsy and not very impressive, it had to be said) pony to such a fate? There was more to a pony than its looks, she thought, remembering all the other stand-offish and unfriendly ponies she had tried. Hannah recalled how much her Spiky pony had seemed to want Hannah to choose him – and Hannah knew exactly how that felt. Could she really have forgotten all that so quickly?

"I haven't given you a chance," Hannah sighed, "and neither has anyone else." She kissed the pony's nose. "Don't worry," she reassured him, "you're not going anywhere. You're going to stay here and be my pony and we'll show them what being partners is all about. You're home, Spiky pony, you're home."

The pony shook his head up and down so that his comical mane wobbled about. *You've got a deal*, he seemed to say. *And you won't regret it!*

Chapter Six

"OH LET HER COME," said Fi, in her well-practised, ever-so-bored voice. She turned Florin towards the gate and Jessica and Ellie followed. Hannah hurried to mount her pony, bobbing up and down on the spot on one leg, the other in the stirrup, as he hurried after the others.

"Spike, wait for me," implored Hannah, but Spike broke into a jog instead, and Hannah just managed to swing her leg over the saddle as he bounced along to catch up.

"You know what you are, Spike," Hannah told him, "you're rude!" Spike nodded his head as if agreeing with her, and they trailed along after Jessica, who in turn trailed along behind Fi and Ellie. Jessica always rode out with Fi and Ellie and had asked whether Hannah could come too. Her new friends were far from enthusiastic about it, and even Jessica seemed a bit off now they were trailing in their wake. Hannah was made up to be part of Fi and Ellie's circle. Her dreams were coming true – not only was she a pony owner, she was a member of the in-crowd.

Sort of.

The hack was not quite as Hannah had imagined it would be. When they cantered along the bridle path Spike, excited by riding out with the other ponies, did a rather good impression of a bouncing ball, and Strawberry Pop went into a strop because he kept bouncing behind her, having already overtaken Roxy.

"Keep him back, Pop's getting very upset!" Ellie squeaked.

"Spike can't go at that dead-slow canter like Pop," Hannah replied, defending him. It wasn't Spike's fault Strawberry Pop could canter on the spot. "He likes to get on!" she added.

"Well let him get on somewhere else, not bouncing off Pop's tail!" Ellie replied. Hannah realised that Strawberry Pop wasn't the perfect pony she had taken her for. Besides getting excited in a crowd and jogging and cantering sideways, Hannah remembered how the strawberry roan pony was fearful of dogs, especially out hacking.

"Perhaps I should go in front?" suggested Hannah.

Fi gave her a withering look. "I don't think so. *As if!*" she said with a snort. Hannah remembered that Fi always said Florin had to go in front or else he had a nut-do. What a pain!

They rode on, Fi and Ellie in front, Jessica and Hannah behind. Spike walked and jogged in turn, looking around at all the unfamiliar sights, tossing his head. Hannah patted his neck – he seemed so delighted to be out and she hoped his enthusiasm would be infectious.

It turned out that it wasn't.

"Honestly Hannah, can't you get Spike to walk properly?" asked Jessica.

"Why?" asked Hannah, looking at Roxy. Jessica's pony just walked on, staring into space. Well behaved but... well... unenthusiastically dull, she thought.

"He's upsetting Roxy," pouted Jessica. Roxy looked anything but upset. Hannah decided Jessica was just trying to sound like Fi. She couldn't understand why as Fi was so superior, and not in a good way. Fi and Ellie were not at all how she imagined they would be when she and Jessica had dreamed of being their friends. They really weren't very friendly at all, but rather seemed to enjoy bossing them both about. It was obvious they considered the new pony owners far inferior to themselves. Hannah realised that Jessica sounded a lot more like Fi when she was at the yard. At school she sounded like her old self but when she was with Fi and Ellie, Hannah had noticed that her friend sounded – and acted – quite differently. Hannah hoped things would change now she was a pony owner and one of the gang. Fi and Ellie would soon be her best chums. It was just a case of everyone getting used to being together, she was sure of it.

The four riders made their way to the top of the hill and stopped for a moment, gazing down at the view below. From here they could see for miles. There was the main road snaking its way through the countryside, the cars and lorries looking like toys. There was the lake with fishermen all around it, like tiny models. There was the riding school with its indoor school and the ponies dotted about in the fields. There were three of the ponies on the wrong side of the fence, trotting away from their home like naughty children playing truant…

"Oh no, look!" exclaimed Jessica, pointing. "The ponies have got out!"

Everyone turned to where she pointed, fully aware of how serious the situation could be. In the field the ponies were safe and unable to nibble on poisonous plants, get stuck in wire carelessly left lying about, injure themselves on farm machinery or stray on to the roads. But outside the field's fencing, well, anything could happen!

"Which ponies are they?" gasped Ellie, leaning up Strawberry Pop's neck and screwing up her eyes.

"I can see Rambo, and the black dot must be Charcoal. I can't see who the third one is," said Hannah.

"It's Nimbus. He was turned out with them this morning because Alice, who owns him, is on holiday," said Fi, pulling her mobile phone out of her pocket. "Oh no, there's no signal – there never is around here! We'll have to go and get them, they're heading for the downs and if they reach the open spaces we'll never catch them!"

"Come on, we're wasting time!" cried Hannah, turning Spike towards the loose ponies.

"Not *you*," snapped Fi. "You go back to the riding school and tell them what's happened. Everyone will panic when they discover the ponies are missing and they won't realise we're on the case."

Hannah had to admit that Fi had a point. And on the plus side she had actually spoken directly to her for a change.

Fi had the annoying habit of talking about her to the others as though she wasn't actually there. Hannah decided she probably wouldn't be much use trying to catch loose ponies anyway. And, as if to seal the deal, Spike bounced about on the spot – he would only get over-excited and mess things up. She didn't want to do anything else wrong today. However…

"But we're not allowed to ride out alone, it's one of the rules," Hannah said.

"Ordinarily, yes, but this is an *eeee-mer-gen-ceee*, so it will be all right," sighed Fi, as though Hannah was the dimmest person on the planet and unable to work anything out for herself.

Reluctantly, Hannah turned Spike in the direction of home, telling herself they had no less an important part to play as rounding up the ponies.

"Okay, good luck," she said.

"She thinks we need luck, not realising that when you have experience with ponies, as Ellie and I do, you don't need luck," sneered Fi, talking as though Hannah wasn't within earshot again.

Oooooh, thought Hannah. Since she'd got to know Fi better there were times when she was tempted to sock her right in the kisser!

Spike cantered along quite willingly away from the others – which surprised Hannah. She thought he wouldn't want to leave them but he shook his head and snorted as if to say, *Thank goodness we're shot of that lot!*

Hannah leant forward and patted his chestnut neck. "They'll come around, Spike," she told him. "We're part of the gang now. We'll all be having great fun soon."

As they were about to leave the hillside and head for the riding school, Hannah turned to see if the loose ponies were still headed towards the downs.

There weren't.

They had turned in another direction completely and were now heading towards the busy main road. No longer trotting, they'd broken into a swift canter.

Hannah gasped and felt her hand fly to her mouth. Not the road! She glanced back behind her but the others had disappeared into the woods and couldn't see the drama laid out before them. For a brief few seconds Hannah stared and wondered what to do. If she carried on back to the riding school it could be too late to do anything, the ponies would reach the road – the terrifyingly busy road where drivers wouldn't be expecting loose ponies. Hannah shut her eyes, imagining what would happen when vulnerable ponies and hurrying vehicles met – flesh-and-blood against speeding iron and steel. It was too awful to think about. Jessica and the others were heading in entirely the wrong direction with no way of knowing that the ponies had changed course. Only Hannah knew – and only Hannah could do anything about it.

But what?

Chapter Seven

LEANING FORWARD, HANNAH GENTLY pulled Spike's
ears. "Spike," she said, as much to herself as to her
pony, "if we carry on back to the yard nobody will be
able to stop the ponies getting to the road. I have to do
something. Maybe we can catch up with the others so they
can change direction – but they've got a head start on us.
We may be too late!"

Aware that every second counted, Hannah still
couldn't make up her mind what to do. She wasn't used to
making decisions. She wasn't used to coping. She was used
to following, not leading. As she sat in the saddle dithering
Spike turned his head and gave Hannah a long look. It
was the sort of look someone gives you when they are a
bit undecided and trying to make up their mind about
something – like telling you a secret, for example. Hannah

had never seen him look at her like that before. The look went right through her and made her feel nervous and thrilled and excited, all at the same time.

Snorting as though he had made a decision, Spike bounced forward into a canter. Hannah had to grab his mane just to stay on.

"Stop, Spike," she gasped, wriggling back into the saddle. "This isn't the direction the others took!" But Spike didn't stop. Instead, he increased his pace and, just when Hannah thought he couldn't possibly go any faster, Spike leapt in the air as though he were jumping a huge, imaginary jump. The air whooshed by Hannah's ears as she heard a loud POW and a zapping sound. The whole world seemed to turn red, then yellow, then green (like traffic lights, thought Hannah) and Hannah had the weirdest sensation of turning inside out before turning outside in again… and then Spike landed on the ground with no sound at all and was galloping faster even than before, the plan to find Fi, Ellie and Jessica forgotten.

Spike was galloping towards the loose ponies and the road!

Oh, thought Hannah, this is what we're doing then, whatever it is.

Then she wondered what they were going to do when they got to the ponies.

Then the thought crossed her mind that the pony beneath her didn't seem quite the same as she remembered. In fact, he seemed very, *very* different indeed. Instead of his usual muddy-grey mane wobbling in all directions, a golden, luscious mane the colour of ripe corn waved in the breeze in front of Hannah. The ears at the top of the mane were a glorious fiery red chestnut colour, and the stride beneath her was the huge galloping stride of a racehorse, not Spike's usual choppy carthorse dance.

And what was going on with her clothes? Instead of her pink jodhpurs and striped top Hannah suddenly realised she was dressed in a purple all-in-one Lycra number, with a black waistcoat, long black boots and black gloves. There was something on her face – she seemed to be peering through a mask, a black mask with eye slits so she could still see. And whatever could she feel and hear flapping around her shoulders? Was she dreaming? Was she mad? Had she fallen off and was lying unconscious in a hospital bed? Unable to answer any of these questions with any confidence, Hannah decided to hang on and see what happened.

What happened was that Spike came to a dramatic, rearing halt at the side of the road (thank goodness, thought Hannah. She had wondered whether he was going to stop! And then she marvelled at the fact that she had sat the rear without a wobble, which she wouldn't have thought possible with her limited riding experience). Lorries and cars sped past and Spike's mane, his new, improved and glamorous mane, swirled around him like an advertisement for pony shampoo. Hannah's own hair, tied back in a smaller ponytail, swirled under her hat. Hannah felt very odd, not like herself at all. Well, she thought, I don't think I am myself – but more to the point, where are the ponies?

Suddenly, she spotted them! They were galloping towards the road – something seemed to have scared them and they didn't look as though they were going to stop, not for anyone or anything. Hannah and Spike (if, indeed, Hannah thought, that's who they still were) would have to turn the ponies before they reached the road and were run over, or caused a terrible accident. It was their only chance!

But how?

Tossing his golden mane Spike let out a deep and rumbling neigh, rearing once more, like a film horse. Hannah sat the rear with ease and wondered again why she didn't fall off. She would have at any other time – but she didn't seem to be Hannah right now, just as Spike wasn't Spike. She had no time to wonder about it any more because they were having quite an effect on the traffic.

Lorry drivers honked, children pressed their noses to car windows. A traffic jam formed – everyone was looking at Hannah and Spike. Except they didn't seem to see Hannah and Spike, they saw... what did they see? As a coach slowed down Hannah spotted their reflection in one of the windows. Her eyebrows shot up into her hat! She saw the most beautiful bright chestnut pony with a golden mane and tail. Instead of his usual wishy-washy legs, Spike had the most glorious chalky-white stockings from above his knees to his glimmering black hooves. And – get this, thought Hannah – his white star was hidden by a small, black mask like Zorro would wear, or a bandit or... Hannah struggled before coming up with the right word – a *superhero*. Spike was no longer Spike, he was... what, or who?

A child wound down a car window and shouted above the din of the engines, "Wow, look! That must be Superpony!"

Superpony? So what did that make Hannah? In her reflection, she could see the letters PG (backwards, naturally) across the waistcoat. PG?

"And that must be Pony Girl," yelled someone else.

"Thank goodness for Superpony and Pony Girl," another voice cheered.

"Are you saving the world?" asked another.

Spike snorted. The loose ponies were approaching – and they were approaching fast. Rambo led the way, charging through the woods like a rhino, Charcoal and Nimbus behind him. Hannah felt her stomach churn, her heart was in her mouth – what if they couldn't stop them? Not all the traffic had slowed – still more raced by in a hurry to get to wherever the drivers were heading, not expecting ponies to run out in front of them.

But Spike took charge. As Rambo galloped towards them through the trees Spike whirled around to face him, rearing and neighing once more like a stallion, his gleaming white forelegs waving in the air. Hannah grabbed his golden mane and waved her hand. She could feel the thing around her shoulders flapping in the breeze. It seemed to billow out like wings. Throwing up his head in amazement Rambo took one horrified look before turning around in a single movement and galloping back the way he'd come, Charcoal and Nimbus hot on his heels. Hannah didn't care where they went – as long as they weren't going to end up squashed flat on the road, and cause a terrible accident in the bargain.

Spike returned to all fours and Hannah realised the flapping thing around her shoulders was a *cape*. She and

Spike really were superheroes – or rather, a superhero and a superheroine. Wow! Hannah the superheroine. Not Hopeless Hannah, but Pony Girl! WOW, WOW, WOW!

"Oh Spike, you're so clever," Hannah told him, entwining her fingers around his golden mane. "And such a dark horse!" she added, her eyebrows rising again.

Spike snorted. She couldn't tell whether he was saying, *Oh, it was nothing*, or *Yes I know!* But there was little time for flattery. Spike reared again and hit the ground at a fast canter, racing after the escaped ponies, leaving the road and the traffic and their cheering public behind. They dodged trees, jumped logs, leapt over streams – and all the while Hannah sat perfectly still, whereas usually she would feel a bit unsafe and have to hold on to the front of her saddle or Spike's mane. Not today, not when she was Pony Girl! She sat in wonder as Spike – Superpony – did everything necessary to save the ponies. All she had to do was stay on board and look the part. They could see the ponies ahead, and soon they were galloping alongside them with Spike guiding them home. As the three ponies trotted into the stable yard at Lavender Riding School everyone came out from the stables to catch them, and Hannah could see their looks of amazement as they spotted her and Spike.

How am I going to explain this, she wondered.

But she didn't have to, because no-one knew who they really were. They called out *Hurrah for Pony Girl*, and *Superpony and Pony Girl have saved the ponies*, and *How can we ever thank you, Pony Girl?* Spike reared again (he seemed to do a lot of that, thought Hannah), and gave a deep neigh before turning and galloping back into the woods, with Hannah sitting tall and proud, her cape billowing out behind her like wings. Then there was another leap in the air, another loud ZAP and POW noise, more lights and the strange inside-out, outside-in feeling, and they were back to being Hannah and Spike again, just as before.

Phew, thought Hannah, not knowing whether to be relieved or sad. She had wondered whether they would have to be Pony Girl and Superpony for ever, but now they were back to normal.

Whatever passed for normal, Hannah thought.

"I think we'll ride around for a while, Spike," she suggested. She wanted to think about their adventure and needed some time to settle herself. She felt elated, and not a little spooked, by the whole experience. It had been so weird, so surreal that now she and Spike were back to their old selves Hannah wondered whether she had dreamt the whole adventure.

When Hannah and Spike finally returned to the yard, Fi, Ellie and Jessica had also got back. Fi was miffed because they had ridden for miles before realising the ponies hadn't gone the way they'd anticipated. Ellie was tired because Strawberry Pop had got thoroughly excited and had refused to walk home, preferring to jog and canter instead, and Jessica was saddle sore – they'd been out for ages. All three wanted to know why Hannah hadn't come back to the yard to tell everyone about the ponies' escape. Everyone's thrilling account of Pony Girl and Superpony just annoyed them even more, and Hannah was called hopeless again.

Only this time, Hannah didn't care.

"Let them think what they like," she whispered to Spike as she settled him for the night. "They don't know that you're Superpony, and even if I told them they'd never believe me. They'd just laugh and think I was making it up."

Hannah laid her head against Spike's cheek, listening to him chewing his hay, remembering how she had felt as Pony Girl, riding her Superpony. It had been like nothing Hannah had ever experienced before. She'd felt – Hannah struggled to find the word – *complete*.

"Will we be Pony Girl and Superpony again, Spike?" Hannah asked, running her fingers through her pony's indecisive mane.

Spike answered by curling himself in half in order to scratch his tummy with his teeth. Except that he almost overbalanced, just managing to save himself in time.

Hannah sighed. Spike was back to being the most clumsy pony on the yard. If they were ever going to be superheroes again, Spike wasn't telling.

Chapter Eight

PONY GIRL AND SUPERPONY were the talk of the riding school – everyone was wondering who they were, where they'd come from and, the biggest question of all, where they had disappeared to after the escaped ponies were safe. What a mystery! Jessica, Fi and Ellie were furious they'd missed all the excitement.

"It's your fault, Hannah," Ellie said, between mouthfuls of cheese-and-onion crisps. "You're hopeless!" Hannah said nothing. What was the point? Her dreams of being one of the gang were seriously on hold because of Fi and Ellie's attitude. She was severely disappointed that their treatment of her was so poor, even though she was now firmly planted on Planet Pony Owner. Would things be different if she had bought the grey or the palomino instead of Spike, she wondered. Hannah couldn't help thinking their attitude would be very different indeed, but part of her doubted it. Now she and Spike were in the livery yard Hannah observed how they treated Jessica – and it wasn't so different to how Fi and Ellie treated her.

When the local newspaper was delivered to her home, Hannah discovered that she and Spike were the talk of the neighbourhood, not just the yard. Or rather, Superpony and Pony Girl were.

Pony Girl and Superpony save motorists from disaster! screamed the headline on the front page. There was a report by the newspaper's roving reporter, an eye-witness account and a not-too-clear photograph of Pony Girl and Superpony, snapped by an onlooker on their mobile phone. Hannah couldn't believe her eyes – there was the most beautiful chestnut pony with a golden mane and tail and chalky-white legs rearing dramatically, and in the saddle was Hannah – or rather, Pony Girl. Is that really me, she wondered. Her hair, instead of its usual mousy colour, was flaming amber, like Superpony's coat, and encased in a ponytail. Her Pony Girl outfit was slinky and close-fitting, the cape billowing around her like a frame. More to the point, Hannah thought, could that amazing pony really be Spike?

Both Pony Girl and Superpony wore small, black masks to hide their identities. No-one would ever, *ever* recognise us anyway, Hannah thought. There was no way anyone would think Pony Girl and Superpony were really Hopeless Hannah and clumsy Spike. She wasn't altogether certain herself. Had she imagined it? No, there was the report in the paper. They had rescued motorists from an inevitable pile-up, said the report. They had arrived in the nick of time, according to the eye-witness, cape swirling, taking charge of the situation (at least, Hannah thought, Superpony had). The ponies would have been killed, along with innocent people in their cars, the newspaper assured its readers. There was much speculation about what might have happened if the dynamic duo hadn't appeared without a second to spare. But they had. They were heroes.

At the bottom of the report was a plea to the public, WHO ARE THESE MASKED SUPERHEROES? Hannah instinctively felt it wouldn't be a good idea to confess. Even if she did, who would believe her? Then she noticed another note at the bottom of the report. *Equine TV star missing – foul play suspected (turn to page six).* Curious, Hannah turned the pages.

Where is Black Diamond?

Black Diamond, talented equine star of the Minster Supermarkets advertisements, has gone missing. His groom discovered his empty stable yesterday morning, and a spokesman for Minster Supermarkets is asking for everyone to look out for the horse.

"There is no way Diamond could have got out and strayed," said the spokesman. "We have to suspect foul play. He is to star in our new Christmas commercial, due to be filmed next month, and we are all very worried."

Police are appealing to members of the public to keep an eye out for any unknown black horses in the area, and to search any unused outbuildings on their premises. Be suspicious of anyone seeking livery or grazing for a black horse, it added. Call this number if you suspect anything. A reward is offered.

Hannah pursed her lips. Black Diamond was a bit of a legend – she'd seen him at the opening of a new Minster Supermarket in town last year and had fallen for the stallion's amazing good looks. TV advertisements showed Black Diamond shopping in a Minster Supermarket, choosing produce which was fresh and healthy, endorsing the shop's traceability and quality. Who could have stolen him, she wondered – for surely someone had.

Fancy, Hannah thought, Spike and I get the front page while poor old Black Diamond is relegated to page six! She couldn't help but be impressed – even though Superpony and Pony Girl were the stars of the show, not Spike and Hannah. Hannah was dying to show Spike his picture in the paper, but didn't dare. Anyway, how mad would she look, showing her pony a newspaper?

When she got to the riding school Spike was waiting for her, head over his stable door, greeting her as usual with a cheerful whinny. Hannah tied him up outside his stable and fetched the mucking out tools. She was getting used to the mess that greeted her every morning: upturned water bucket, hay mixed into the wood chippings, holes dug out of the bedding. It was as though her pony was trying to tunnel his way out. As usual, Spike seemed to be wearing more bedding than was left on the floor, and Hannah set to work tidying up and mucking out.

"Whoa!" cried a voice, and Hannah looked up to see Joshua in the doorway. "Looks like a war zone in there," he added.

"I suppose Rambo's morning bed is immaculate!" said Hannah, fed up with constant criticism.

"It's not as bad as this," Joshua replied. "Have you had any more thoughts about hogging that pony's mane?" he asked.

Hannah cursed under her breath. She had meant to put Spike's mane in plaits to train it. She vowed to do it after mucking out. "No," she replied, "because I'm not going to. I'm going to train it to fall on one side."

"Really? Good luck with that!" said Joshua. "By the way, how are you getting on with the little princesses?" he asked.

"Who?" asked Hannah, mystified.

"Princess Fi and Princess Ellie," explained Joshua.

"Er, fine," said Hannah, not wishing to appear rude about Fi and Ellie, but thinking how Joshua had managed to sum up the pair of them exactly. "Why do you call them that?" she asked, innocently.

"Oh, no reason," said Joshua, and he winked before sauntering off down the row of stables to see Rambo.

Hannah emptied the wheelbarrow, re-laid Spike's bed and filled the water bucket, comforted to know that she wasn't the only one who had noticed Fi and Ellie's attitude. Hanging up a small net of hay outside, she tied Spike next to it before collecting her grooming box.

"Now Spike," she said, climbing on a stool so she was level with his mane, "you want a nice, tidy mane, don't you? I'm going to make that happen."

With some difficulty (Spike kept tearing at the hay net, nodding his head and turning around to talk to her in a friendly way), Hannah managed to put her pony's mane into fourteen plaits on the offside of his neck.

"There," she said, struggling to fasten a plait band around the very last one as Spike was ticklish and his withers kept shuddering like an angry jelly, "that should do it! You've got such a lot of mane, Spike. Once it's trained over I'll pull it shorter so it looks really neat." Hannah wasn't entirely certain her pony didn't shoot her a look which said, *that's what you think*, but she told herself she'd imagined it. We'll show Joshua, she thought.

Standing back and assessing her work, Hannah had to admit that the plaits weren't the neatest she'd ever seen. After all, she'd had to force more than half the mane over to a side it didn't want to go so the plaits veered off in all directions – some down, some up, some right, some left. She acknowledged that taming it might take a while. Hannah groomed Spike before putting him back into his stable and returning her grooming kit to the tack room. She'd only been gone long enough to get her saddle, bridle and riding hat but when she returned Spike had rubbed out no fewer than three plaits, leaving the mane which had been in them tangled and broken.

"Whatever are you doing with Spike's mane?" asked Jessica, who had just arrived. "Isn't it odd-looking enough?"

Hannah wondered what was happening to her friend. She never used to be so, so... well, like Fi and Ellie, Hannah thought. She explained the plaits, repairing the rubbed ones as best she could.

"You could hog it," suggested Jessica.

"Have you been talking with Joshua?" Hannah asked her.

Jessica went a bit pink. "Rambo looks really good hogged," she said, a little too quickly. Hannah was aware that Spike had stopped chewing hay and was holding his breath.

"I don't want Spike hogged," Hannah said, firmly. Spike resumed his chewing.

"Suit yourself," said Jessica, moving on to see Roxy. Hannah turned back to her own pony.

"You need to stop rubbing out these plaits otherwise you may *have* to be hogged," she told him. "Once you've rubbed out your mane, I'll have no choice!" Spike gave her a solemn stare before frisking her pockets for sweets, and Hannah gave him a kiss, tacked him up and went for a ride.

Chapter Nine

HANNAH PARTICULARLY WANTED TO ride out alone. She knew she wasn't supposed to – the yard had a strict policy that no-one should – but she felt the need to be alone with Spike so she sneaked out while everyone was busy. Besides, she told herself, nobody ever took any notice of them so it was doubtful they'd be missed, and they wouldn't be out for long. She had the feeling that Spike would never turn into Superpony when they were riding with the others, and she was quite desperate to become Pony Girl again. She had felt so very different when she had been Pony Girl, not at all like herself. Usually she felt awkward, hesitant, quite unsure about what she was doing – constantly wondering whether she was doing things the right way, the way others would do things, the way they might approve.

Hannah wasn't confident like Fi and Ellie – how she wished she was. She had always wondered what it would be like to be the sort of person who was sure of themselves, a person other people wanted to be like. Hannah knew exactly how it felt to be a person other people *didn't* want to be like. During her brief stint as Pony Girl Hannah had felt as though she had nothing to prove to anyone. She'd felt like she could do anything – and do it well. It had been a feeling she had never experienced before and she wanted to feel it again. Oh how desperately she wanted to feel like that again!

Hannah steered Spike through the woods and out towards the open fields. It was early, she could hear the birds singing and there was no sign of anyone else riding. Patting her pony's neck Hannah leant forward and whispered in his ear. "Hey Spike, can we be Pony Girl and Superpony again please?"

Nothing happened. Spike kept walking purposefully and noiselessly over the grass, his ears flicking back and forth at the sound of Hannah's voice. Hannah tried again.

"Come on Spike, please! It'll be fun. We can save someone or something. I know you can do it!"

Spike snorted and tossed his head. Hannah's heart sank, realising it was no use. She had no influence over Spike. She wondered whether he would ever transport her into their alternative lives again. She even began to wonder whether she had imagined their adventure. Just because the report was in the paper, it didn't mean that she, Hannah, was Pony Girl. Maybe she had just wanted it to be her. Maybe someone else was Pony Girl. Probably Fi,

Hannah thought despondently, that would be just about right.

But how she wanted it to be true! Hannah wanted it more than anything. More than she wanted to win rosettes. More than owning a pony other people would be jealous of. More, even – and this one surprised her – than being good at something and being picked for a team. She wanted it because of how it had made her feel, because how she had felt when she'd been Pony Girl meant that winning rosettes or being good at something no longer mattered. Goodness, thought Hannah, the possibility of never having that feeling back again was just unimaginable. What if it *never* happened again? How would she cope with that? She just *had* to relive that feeling!

Hannah was so lost in her thoughts that she and Spike rode on through more fields, and then woods, and soon she no longer recognised where she was. They hadn't followed a bridle path, so simply turning around and retracing their steps wasn't an option. Halting in a clearing, Hannah looked around her. If I were good at geography, she thought, I'd have taken notice of the sun's position and known which way to head back. Of course, that plan would work better if the sun was actually out, instead of the day being cloudy and grey, she decided, so being rubbish at geography didn't really matter. She had her mobile on her but didn't dare phone the yard. There would be hell to pay if Mrs Evans discovered she was riding alone. Besides, she noted with a sinking feeling of irony, she must be ages away from the riding school as her mobile was showing she had good network coverage, which proved how far they'd come. Even if she did call she had no idea where she was, which wasn't very helpful for anyone trying to find her.

"I suppose you know the way back, Spike," Hannah said, dropping the reins so her pony could take her home, like ponies do in books and in films. Spike answered by dropping his head and tearing at the grass. Sighing, Hannah pulled his head up again and urged him in the direction a hunch drew her. After half-an-hour, she pulled up again.

"I believe we are even loster," she told Spike, fully aware that there was no such word. Spike sighed but then, cheerful as ever, set off purposefully in another direction. Excited to think that her pony knew the way home Hannah's spirits lifted – before tumbling once more as Spike stopped at a tasty bush and nibbled at the leaves.

"You know," Hannah began, in a persuading voice, "I bet Superpony could save us. After all, we are totally lost and we do need saving. And it looks like rain," she added, noticing that the clouds had turned a darker shade of grey. Spike just kept nibbling leaves, his snaffle bit jangling around ever-increasing green slime.

"Come on," sighed Hannah gathering up her reins once more. "We need to find a landmark."

Riding on for another ten minutes or so, the duo emerged from a wood into a small hamlet of houses around a church. Riding up to the church gate, Hannah read the sign.

"St Peter's, Wends Ditton," she said aloud. "Never heard of it. Oh," she continued, seeing a woman walking her dog, "excuse me, do you know how I might get back to Great Lytherston?"

"You ridden all the way over from there?" asked the woman, unnecessarily, thought Hannah, nodding.

"Goodness, that's a long way!" said the woman. "I've a friend who lives there and it takes me a while by car!"

Neither interesting, thought Hannah, nor an answer to her question.

"Of course, it's a lot shorter across country..." continued the woman. Her black Labrador stood beside her with its tongue hanging out, its tail wagging, staring into the distance and probably dreaming of biscuits. "... and quite a nice ride, I expect. You on your own?"

"Yes. Do you know the way back?" Hannah asked again with more urgency, feeling a few drops of rain on her face. Spike shook his head, his plaits pinging around his neck.

"Not by pony," said the woman. "I'll ask Dorothy, she might know." Pulling out her mobile phone she dialled a number. After confirming that she was fine, thanks, and that Tom was as well as to be expected after his operation, and that she was indeed on flower duty at the church this Saturday and would see her there – there would be plenty to do as there was a wedding booked for the afternoon, Pricilla's eldest and her lovely young man – only she may be late as she had to wait in for someone to come and look at the washing machine which had broken down and yes, the laundry was piling up, couldn't come a moment too soon and they wouldn't give her a definite time, as usual, just between nine and twelve, as if she had nothing else to do but stay in and wait for them, the woman finally got around to asking Dorothy Hannah's question.

Following a good many nods of the head and a great many *oh rights*, the woman ended her call and pointed back towards where Hannah had come from, telling her to follow the line of trees around the fields, pick up the path through the woods until she got to the stream, to turn left there, right at the fallen gate and then she'd be on the right bridle path for Great Lytherston. With her head swimming with all the instructions Hannah headed Spike in the direction of the pointed finger, the rain upgrading from a few spots into a fully-blown downpour as soon as they got to the woods.

Two hours later, a very wet Hannah and Spike arrived back at the yard where Hannah was immediately summoned to Mrs Evans' office to explain why she had gone riding alone, and to apologise to all the people who had been sent out riding in the rain to find her, as Mrs Evans had been convinced she was lying in a ditch somewhere. Hannah almost blurted out that there had been no need to worry as she'd had Superpony with her, before realising that would not only make things worse, but confirm she was pretty weird. Besides, Hannah thought, she was no longer totally convinced about Superpony as Spike had made no attempt to save her. It must all have been a dream after all.

"Whatever possesses one to go riding alone," sneered Fi, her blonde hair shining in a particularly superior manner. "Everyone knows we're not allowed. And inexperienced riders in particular shouldn't do it. I mean, some people are a liability, not to mention their odd ponies."

"It's not like you have the experience Fi and I have," chipped in Ellie, throwing another spent crisp bag in the bin. "I mean, you're practically a beginner rider, and that pony of yours is totally bonkers."

"Spike's totally reliable!" cried Hannah, defending her pony. "He's a lot more reliable than Strawberry Pop!"

"Oh that is so totally untrue," gasped Ellie. "I don't know how you can even compare my talented jumper to your loser of a pony. I mean, he can't even walk in a straight line!"

"At least he doesn't go into meltdown when he sees a dog, like Strawberry Pop does," replied Hannah, thoroughly wound up.

"It's not her fault, she was attacked by a dog when she was a foal!" screamed Ellie, and Hannah felt a bit bad because, obviously, nobody wants to hear something like that.

"Ignore her Ellie," said Fi, taking her friend by the arm. "Don't have anything to do with her, she's as mad as her pony. In fact, they're a total match, both *exaaaaactly* the same. Come on Jessica, we don't want anything more to do with Hopeless Hannah and that Spiky pony of hers."

Hannah looked on aghast as Jessica's eyes widened. She could see her friend was torn between loyalty to Hannah, and the thrill of being part of Fi and Ellie's circle. With a shoulder shrug, which Hannah took to mean she thought her friend had brought it upon herself, Jessica turned and followed Fi and Ellie. Hannah felt more hurt than she could have imagined. Blinking back tears of disappointment and rage she ran into Spike's stable, burying her head into her pony's neck, the plaits pressing into her forehead.

"Oh Spike," whispered Hannah, wiping her tears away with her sleeve, "all I wanted was to be one of the gang and I thought having my own pony would do it. I'm still useless at everything – even making friends – and it doesn't look as though I'm ever going to be Pony Girl again, if indeed I ever was. Where did it all go so wrong?"

Spike nuzzled her between mouthfuls of hay. *Cheer up!* he seemed to say. *We don't need them. We're a team, remember?* But this time, even Spike's cheerfulness didn't lift Hannah, and in her disappointment she couldn't help wondering whether she'd made the right choice, and whether a palomino or dappled grey pony would have earned her the standing she so craved. She didn't want to admit it but the words which had hurt the most were Fi's. She was right, she and Spike were the same. She had longed for a pony which would enable her to be hopeless no more, a pony who would help her become a person who could do something well and leave Hopeless Hannah behind. It seemed she had blown that – getting Spike had blown it. She had bought a pony which was just like her. She and Spike were as much of a match as Fi and Florin, Ellie and Strawberry Pop, Jessica and Roxy. She had been right at the dealer's yard, Spike had wanted to be chosen for her team, just as she always wanted to be chosen – and never was. They were a perfectly-matched pair.

In her misery Hannah wondered again whether she'd been right to buy Spike – and then remembered, with a feeling of disloyalty, what might have happened to him if she hadn't, and how he had made her feel when he had turned into Superpony, and she into Pony Girl. But that didn't help because it seemed the Pony Girl thing wasn't happening again either. Hannah didn't know which felt worse – her disappointment or her guilt.

Chapter Ten

HANNAH LOOKED AT THE timetable with mounting dread. Double PE was the last lesson of the day. Might as well be double torture, thought Hannah, changing into her PE kit.

"Rounders today girls!" declared Miss Craig in her customary, over bright manner, her dark hair tied back in a band, track suit zipped up to her chin. Carrie and Eleanor, choose teams please, quickly!"

Hannah's heart sank. As names were shouted out and friends rushed to secure their places on the teams her mind wandered back to Spike and how alike they were. Hostile faces greeted her as, last to be picked as usual, she dawdled over to Carrie's team.

"You're fielding – and *run* this time!" growled Carrie, a strapping girl for whom batting, throwing, swimming, cycling, running and jumping were second nature. Whenever talent failed her, she made up any deficit with brute force. Hannah made her way to the far end of the sports field, hoping not to be troubled by the ball. She watched the others batting, running, throwing, congratulating each other, high-fiving. Positioned at third base, Jessica got three players on the opposing team out. Hannah didn't mind fielding as she could just stay out of the way, as instructed. It was when she came to bat things got tricky.

"Okay girls, change over!" came the instruction after Miss Craig blew her whistle half-way through the session. Hannah dawdled over to stand in line, watching her team mates hit the ball and run from base to base. Jessica got a rounder. The line grew shorter. There were three people in front of Hannah. Then two. Then one.

"Just look at the ball and try to hit it!" hissed Carrie, giving her a push. What does she think I do, wondered Hannah, taking the bat and facing the bowler. Eleanor gave her a steely glare, hurling the ball in a well-executed throw. The ball lifted in the air, seeming to grow as it sailed towards her, and Hannah gripped the bat tightly.

Here it comes, I can hit it, I'm going to hit it this time! thought Hannah, and she saw her right arm go forward to meet the ball with a loud *thwack*, propelling it past Eleanor's ear, a hundred metres over the grass, way beyond the fielders, bouncing towards the school fence. Hannah heard a loud, collective gasp from the whole class as she threw the bat behind her and ran, ran, ran, scoring an easy rounder to the enthusiastic cheer from her team who rallied around her, thumping her on the back and singing her praises.

Except that it was all in her mind…

"*OUT!*" screamed the backstop behind her as the ball rose upwards from the merest glance from Hannah's bat and sailed gracefully down into waiting hands.

Hannah was aware of the resigned groans, the rolling eyes of her team members. She went and sat down on the grass, agreeing with Carrie when she heard her say in an unnecessarily loud voice that it was just as well Hopeless Hannah was out of the way. Would she ever be good at anything? On the bright side, she had at least brushed the ball with the bat. Usually, she didn't get anywhere near it, just swung through thin air.

Hannah couldn't wait to get changed and rush to the stables to see Spike. She felt terrible about her feelings at the yard the day before and wanted to make it up to him. He really was such a nice pony, she thought. Okay, he wasn't perfect but hadn't she just demonstrated that she was anything but perfect herself? Who was she to judge? Plus, he was the only person on the planet who ever seemed happy to see her.

Hannah's heart sank when she saw Fi and Ellie grooming their ponies in the yard. Although they saw her arrive they pointedly ignored her, exchanging glances with each other. Grabbing Spike's head collar, Hannah ran to the field to catch him. Several ponies, including Roxy, stood near the gate waiting for their owners, but Spike was nowhere to be seen.

I hope he hasn't got out, thought Hannah, her heart sinking. But he hadn't. Walking to the far end of the field, where the ponies could hide in the gorse bushes, Hannah found her pony grazing with the riding school's grey donkey, Moke. When he saw her Spike whinnied a friendly greeting, making Hannah feel even more guilty.

"Come on, Spike," she called as both he and Moke watched her approach. The donkey was ancient – word was that Mrs Evans had learnt to ride on him back in the day – and spent his days grazing alone, ignored by all the ponies. Hannah had never really taken much notice of Moke – he'd just always been in the field, bothering no-one, no-one bothering him. Now it seemed her pony had taken a shine to him. They seemed, she observed, the best of chums. As if to underline her suspicions Spike and Moke began mutually grooming each other – each biting the other's neck to scratch all the itchy bits they couldn't reach themselves, a favour only bestowed by real equine friends.

Please don't let Moke be your new bezzie mate, thought Hannah, sighing. It would be typical, she thought, for Spike to pal up with the only donkey in the field, the donkey nobody else took any notice of. At least Fi and Ellie hadn't seen.

"You really don't help yourself, do you!" she scolded him, struggling to fasten Spike's head collar as he continued to nibble Moke's fluffy neck. Moke followed them as she led Spike to the gate and looked on wistfully, his long ears flapping back and forth as his new best mate was led away and into the yard.

"Oh, here he is, Moke's new best friend!" giggled Fi, placing her snow-white saddle cloth on Florin's golden back and crushing Hannah's belief that her pony's best chum was still a secret.

"They're a perfect match," sniggered Ellie, oiling Strawberry Pop's hooves so they glistened in the sunlight. "Donkeys should stick together!"

"Can I come riding with you?" Jessica asked them breathlessly, arriving late. "I had to stay after school but it won't take me long to get Roxy and tack her up."

"Well, only if you're *veeeeery* quick," said Fi. "But we can't always wait for you."

"Thanks, I'll be two ticks, honest!" promised Jessica, grabbing Roxy's head collar and running towards the field.

She could have ridden with me, thought Hannah. Whatever had happened to her friend? She was still *The Traitor Jessica*, she thought. Nobody had asked Hannah whether she wanted to join them. She appeared to be totally out of the loop. She could ask them, she thought. She decided not to. She didn't enjoy riding with them as they were just so superior, and made her feel worse about herself.

Spike dragged her into his stable and inspected his manger, displaying disappointment when it proved to be empty.

"Sorry," said Hannah, raiding her pockets for a carrot. She was a bad pony owner, she thought, and she had to pull up her socks. Spike was her pony, there was no going back and she did really love him, despite her recent thoughts. At least he was a genuine friend. As she watched Fi, Ellie and Jessica all ride out of the yard Hannah wondered what she was going to do. She didn't want to ride in the school and she didn't need reminding about riding alone. She was stuck.

"Going riding?" said a voice. It was Joshua, already mounted on Rambo.

"I was," said Hannah, "but I've no-one to ride with."

"Me too," Joshua said. "I don't suppose you'd like to ride out with me? My usual riding chum, Cameron from Orange Tree Stables, is on holiday."

Hannah was astonished. Ride out with Joshua? She imagined the look on Jessica's face when she told her: *'Yeah, that's right, me and Josh went riding. Yeah, it was pretty good, we had a laugh. Going again tomorrow…'*

"Well?" said Joshua.

"Yes, er, okay. I'll get my tack."

Hannah was aware of the surprised reaction of the other livery owners as she and Joshua rode out of the yard together. Rambo marched on, purposeful as ever, and Spike jiggled and jogged from side-to-side, purpose*less* as ever. Hannah tried to keep a lid on her emotions. She was riding out with Joshua. Wow! It looked like her dream about becoming accepted by her peers was coming true at last!

Chapter Eleven

H ANNAH'S DREAM CAME TO an abrupt end when they reached the woods.

"I'm heading up to Litten's Point, I'll be about an hour," said Joshua, reining in Rambo and shifting in the saddle. "There's no point us both going on together and I expect you have your own plans. As long as we're seen to leave and arrive back together everyone at the yard will be none the wiser, don't you agree? I mean, we've both got our mobiles if anything crops up, so there shouldn't be a problem."

"Oh, er, um, yes," mumbled Hannah, realising she'd been well and truly used. Everyone knew mobile phone reception was virtually non-existent in the area – another reason why no-one was supposed to ride alone. She didn't dare say so, she was afraid it would make her sound needy.

"Why don't we meet back here in an hour, then we can ride into the yard together and everyone will be happy?" Joshua suggested. Hannah nodded and turned Spike. Giving him a kick, they cantered away from Joshua and Rambo, Hannah too annoyed at Joshua – and herself – to give way to tears.

"What a colossal nerve!" she said aloud. Spike's ears swivelled in sympathy. At least he didn't care about being on his own, thought Hannah. Some ponies napped and refused to go anywhere without the company of another pony, but Spike didn't mind at all. Hannah patted his neck in gratitude.

Making sure she took notice of where she was riding this time, Hannah rode on. As she rode she began to forget about wanting to be in with Fi and Ellie and Jessica – or even Joshua. She began instead to enjoy being with her pony.

"I'd rather it was just you and me, Spike," she said. "You're better company than the gruesome sisters and the traitor, and much better than some boy who just uses us to get out of the yard."

Reaching a crossroads on the bridle path, Hannah decided to go left. The path wound around in a circle and would bring them back to the meeting point with Joshua at about the right time. But Spike didn't want to go that way. Snorting and tossing his head he turned instead to the opposite direction, planting his feet and refusing to obey his rider.

"I was just thinking how good you were," Hannah scolded him. "You've never napped before. Whatever is the matter, Spike?"

For an answer, Spike trotted off in the direction he wanted to go and Hannah had no choice but to go with him, tugging on the reins in an effort to slow him down and regain some control. But instead of slowing down, Spike went faster. He broke into a canter, then a gallop and as the wind whistled past Hannah's ears he leapt into the air. Hannah heard a POW and a zapping sound, saw red, yellow and green lights flash before her eyes, felt herself turn inside-out and outside-in again, and when they landed she was once again aboard Superpony, looking at two neat amber ears pricked forward, peeping out above locks of golden mane which tumbled around his chestnut shoulders.

Hannah felt like she might explode, she was so elated. She *hadn't* been dreaming, she *was* Pony Girl! Once again she was wearing her Pony Girl outfit, complete with little black mask and swirling cape. The familiar feeling of being whole and complete overwhelmed her as Spike, AKA Superpony, galloped on, eating up the ground, carrying them to goodness-knows-where, on to another adventure. Hannah felt like laughing and singing, both at the same time!

Hannah couldn't tell how long they galloped – it may have been seconds, minutes or an hour – but Superpony finally dropped back to a trot, then a walk, in a place unknown to his rider. They found themselves outside a farmyard which was very rundown. A huge barn held scattered hay bales, old and mouldy. A tractor rusted quietly by the entrance and a sign declaring the place to be *Home Farm* swung desolately from one nail, creaking in the wind. There was no sign of life – no chickens, no ducks, no dogs, no people.

Hannah would never have entered such a place and would have ridden straight past but Pony Girl was curious. Why had Superpony brought her here? The pair walked on to the yard and Superpony came to a halt outside a brick building. Weeds grew between the bricks, and the rotting roof and stagnant puddles reflected the decay. Superpony stood still, his head high, listening. Pony Girl listened too, straining her ears. What were they supposed to hear?

Suddenly, Superpony whirled around and carried Pony Girl at the gallop to the other side of the building – and only just in time. The large door to the brick building opened and a man walked out into the sunshine, a sausage roll in one hand, a can of beer in the other. Dressed in denim, he peered around the yard suspiciously with narrowed eyes. Hidden behind a tree, Superpony and Pony Girl watched. Then Hannah heard something which made sense of everything: a whinny, shrill and desperate, a horse lonely and afraid, a horse in trouble. And Pony Girl knew only one horse would make such a desperate sound.

"Black Diamond!" she gasped, grabbing a lock of Superpony's luxuriant mane. At the back of her mind she couldn't help wondering how long it would take for her plaits to work their magic on Spike, and whether her efforts would ever be rewarded with such a beautiful crowning glory, but she swiftly re-focused on the present – she and Superpony had work to do!

Deciding she needed to do something, Hannah pulled out her mobile – it was still there, thank goodness. She should call the police – except that she hadn't a clue where she and Superpony actually were. How could the police come and rescue Black Diamond, the high-profile equine celebrity, missing from Minster Supermarkets, if they didn't know where to go? She'd have to resort to Plan B. What was Plan B, she wondered. She didn't have long to ponder for the man had replaced the sausage roll with his own mobile phone and was talking loudly enough for her to hear.

"Hurry up, Harry, this place gives me the creeps," he said, looking around him. "How far away are you? This blooming 'orse is getting restless. Can't you hear it neighing? It'll give the game away for sure. What? I daren't give it any more of them sedatives, it was out for the count last time. It's no use to us dead, is it? I've not done all this for meat money, I want my share of that million quid! Get that horsebox here sharpish so we can move it again."

So that was the game, thought Hannah. Ransom! Black Diamond had been horse-napped and it seemed the horse-nappers were going to move him. She had to think and act fast. She wasn't used to thinking and acting fast. Or even thinking and acting, full stop.

But Superpony thought and acted for her. Leaping from their hiding place, he bore down upon the man in denim who dropped both his phone and his beer in terror and ran back into the brick building, screaming as though all the demons in hell were after him instead of just a girl on a pony. Following him, Hannah saw Black Diamond, his head collar tied to a ring in the wall, and was relieved to see that he looked bright and wide awake – she was afraid he'd be sleepy from sedatives.

Grasping a pitchfork, the man in denim faced them, swearing loudly. Hannah caught her breath. This was a serious development she hadn't bargained for, but before she could think of what to do about it, Superpony reared up on his hind legs and boxed the pitchfork right out of the man's hands. Shouting, the man backed off and continued to issue threats as Superpony, snorting and rearing, kept him at bay. Hannah decided she had to do something, she couldn't leave everything to Superpony. Slithering out of the saddle she ran over and untied Black Diamond, patting his neck reassuringly, ignoring the fact that he was so big and impressive, the sort of horse of which she would usually be a little afraid.

"Come on Black Diamond," she whispered, "we've come to rescue you," and she led him outside, calling to Superpony who galloped after her, leaving the man in denim to struggle after them all. Remounting quicker than she ever had in her life, Hannah as Pony Girl sat easily as the trio turned as one and fled the scene. Holding Black Diamond's lead rope tightly Hannah didn't dare look back, fearing what the man in denim might do.

As they galloped towards the gateway and freedom, a horsebox rumbled in, blocking their path. Superpony and Black Diamond were forced to come to a sliding halt, before turning to find another way to escape from what had become a prison for them all.

"Oi, where do you think you're going with that 'orse?" cried the horsebox driver, a large man with a ginger beard, who leapt down from the cab and ran, puffing, towards them.

They were trapped. The yard was old but it was fenced by a solid-looking brick wall and a thick hedge. Hannah caught her breath – what could they do? But she had underestimated Superpony and Black Diamond. Gathering speed they both galloped toward the hedge and, as they reached it, before Hannah could even think about what was going to happen, she felt Superpony gather his legs underneath him and launch himself into space, the dark shadow of Black Diamond matching him stride-for-stride. For a glorious moment Hannah felt as though they were flying (she had never jumped anything so big before but she felt perfectly safe on Superpony), and then they landed, the horses' hooves beating in rhythm as they galloped over the fields away from the shouting men, away from the stable yard and towards the safety of the woods.

Chapter Twelve

HANNAH HAD NO IDEA how she, Superpony and
Black Diamond found their way to a police station
– it was all Superpony's doing. With Black Diamond
taken into protective custody by a worried-looking police
woman, more police were dispatched to Home Farm to
arrest the men who had horse-napped the famous equine
star. Long gone, they were picked up later that night at
Dover, about to drive the horsebox onto a ferry bound for
France. Luckily, Pony Girl had remembered the number
plate. It was something Hannah knew she would never
have been able to do, but when she was Pony Girl she
wasn't herself.

A crowd gathered outside the police station. People
from Minster Supermarkets were soon on the scene,
overjoyed about the return of their legendary celebrity

equine and, of course, the press duly arrived, thrusting a microphone in Pony Girl's face and demanding to know how she and Superpony had found Black Diamond. Hannah would have stuttered and stammered her way through an incomprehensible jumble of words, but to her surprise Pony Girl gave an eloquent statement, giving Superpony full credit and concluding by saying she was only pleased that justice had been done, and she hoped other horse-nappers would think twice while she and Superpony were around. The confident and capable Pony Girl was exactly how Hannah wanted to be – knew she should be – but wasn't. She was totally made up in her new role.

It didn't last, of course. Eventually she sensed that Superpony was restless and anxious to be off and she mounted her stunning equine hero to be whisked away in a trice, to groans from her fans outside the police station who had demanded selfies. Galloping towards home Superpony once more made one of his astonishing leaps, the air whooshed, the inside-out, outside-in thing happened again and Hannah and Spike found themselves in the woods by the stables.

Hannah slid out of the saddle and gave Spike a hug. "That was amazing!" she told him. "Why can't we be Pony Girl and Superpony all the time?" Spike just nuzzled her shoulder in a chummy way, leaving snot on her jumper. How different he was when he was Superpony, Hannah thought. As Superpony his white stockings glinted in the sunlight, his mane and tail swirled like waves. His chestnut coat shone so brightly, Hannah fancied she could see her own amazing Pony Girl reflection in it. Far from being clumsy like Spike, Superpony was graceful and composed. He was like an amazing Hollywood film horse, glamorous, strong, heroic. But now he was Spike again – with a dull brown coat, watery pale legs, plaits sticking out in all directions. They still weren't lying flat, Hannah noticed. They'd been in for days but Spike's mane still did what it wanted to do. It was untameable.

Shutting thoughts of her pony's unsuccessful plaits out of her head Hannah decided she'd concentrate on remembering how it felt to be Pony Girl. High on the thrill of it all Hannah mounted Spike and headed homeward, smiling like an idiot and wrapped up in her own, amazing Pony Girl and Superpony world as she rode into the yard.

Where all hell broke loose.

"Don't tell me you've been RIDING ON YOUR OWN AGAIN!" screamed Mrs Evans. Even Spike's ears flattened onto his neck, his eyes widening at the sound of her voice.

"Er, I can explain..." began Hannah, realising at once that she couldn't. She couldn't tell Mrs Evans about being Pony Girl, or rescuing Black Diamond and being a superhero. She couldn't even tell her she'd started out riding with Joshua and Rambo before being dumped, because then she'd be a tell-tale. Not only had she been out alone, she'd been out for *ages* – Mrs Evans had sent other riders out to try and find her again, including Fi, Ellie and Jessica, who looked daggers at Hannah. Fi was actually standing with her arms folded, tapping a toe.

"If this happens one more time, Hannah Pearson, you'll be looking for a new place to keep that pony of yours," threatened Mrs Evans, wagging a finger in her direction. "I can't have the rules of the yard flaunted so disgracefully. They apply to everyone – including YOU!"

"I'm really sorry, Mrs Evans," said Hannah, arranging her features in what she hoped passed for crestfallen. Even Mrs Evans' shouting couldn't crush her feelings of elation after her amazing adventure. She could rant and rave all she wanted – she, Hannah, was Pony Girl, and Mrs Evans didn't realise how wonderful it was to ride Superpony. Besides, thought Hannah, all superheroes had to keep their true identity secret, everyone knew that. It was the superhero rule.

Unsaddling Spike in his stable Hannah could hear Fi, Ellie and Jessica outside in the yard, talking loudly for her benefit.

"Honestly, that girl is her own *wooooorst* enemy," Fi said. Hannah could picture her with her nose in the air, her blonde locks bobbing around her shoulders, sneering towards Spike's stable.

"How stupid do you have to be to go riding alone twice, when everyone knows the rules," added Ellie, followed by the crunch of a crisp. "Not to mention how we were press-ganged into trying to find her – like we haven't got other things to do."

"She'll be thrown out if she does it again," said Jessica, copying Ellie's indignant, self-righteous tone. Hannah couldn't believe how her friend changed when she was in Fi and Ellie's company.

"Well wouldn't that be a shame," said Fi, and the others giggled. "I think the only person who would mind is Moke, and even he might be grateful not to have that odd pony hanging around him any more."

Hannah heard it all. But whereas previously she'd been troubled by Fi, Ellie and Jessica's remarks, today she didn't care. She and Spike had enjoyed the most terrific adventure as Pony Girl and Superpony and she had felt on top of the world. What did Fi, Ellie and Jessica know?

"Where were you?" Joshua stuck his head over Spike's stable door, looking like thunder. "I had to unsaddle Rambo and pretend I'd been grazing him in-hand to avoid getting a dressing-down when I returned alone – I waited ages for you. My saddle's scratched where I had to hide it in the hedge and Rambo's bit is all green and slimy. You were supposed to meet me where we agreed. How dim are you?"

Usually, Hannah would have turned puce and apologised for letting Joshua down. But today she felt different – Pony Girl feelings lingered.

"You used me, so I don't believe you have a leg to stand on," she said, her eyes flashing. "Perhaps you'll think twice before using me again!"

Joshua's eyes opened wide in surprise. Being the only boy on the yard, all the other girls always hung on his every word so Hannah's reaction was totally alien to him. His mouth opened to say something back – only he couldn't think of anything, so he shut it again and walked off in a huff.

Wow, thought Hannah. She hardly ever dared to speak back to someone. She expected to feel a bit wobbly about it but she didn't. In fact, she felt elated.

"What a cheek!" she told Spike, brushing out the mark his saddle had left on his back. Spike nodded his head up and down as if he agreed and Hannah laughed. "Come on," she said, leading him out of the stable and past Fi, Ellie and Jessica, "let's see if your mate Moke is waiting for you."

He was. Far from being embarrassed, Hannah was glad Spike had a friend – a real friend. And, she acknowledged, as the pair of them walked off to the far side of the field, it was totally awesome that at last, Moke had a friend, too.

Chapter Thirteen

OF COURSE, SUPERPONY AND Pony Girl were all over the newspapers and TV. Hannah looked at the pictures of herself and Spike – they looked so, well different, obviously. Was it really them? It was difficult to believe. But there she was, on the TV, giving an interview – all poised and media-savvy. Amazing! And as for Spike, well, he was the most glamorous pony ever – flowing golden tresses, his head high, his tail brushing the ground. He looked absolutely the pony of Hannah's dreams, the pony everyone would be jealous of.

And they were.

"Superpony is so dreamy," she heard Fi say to Ellie and Jessica as they sat in the tack room, passing the newspaper around and drooling over her pony.

"I wish I were Pony Girl," sighed Jessica. "I *love* her outfit!"

"It would be totally amazing," agreed Ellie. "I wonder who she is? There's a piece here in the paper about it, asking if anyone knows her true identity."

"You can't keep an amazing pony like that a secret," said Fi, matter-of-factly. "If Superpony were in our yard, we'd certainly know about it. He's *sooooo* distinctive."

Hannah smiled to herself. Little did they know that Superpony was stabled next to Roxy, right under their noses. They thought they knew everything, but they didn't know that!

"Maybe he doesn't look like that all the time," she couldn't help saying. Fi turned her head as though she had only just realised Hannah was there.

"Hmmm, you could be right... I suppose he might look like, let me see... *Spike!*" Fi said, and she, Ellie and Jessica roared with laughter. Hannah thought Jessica's laugh didn't sound genuine – more like she was just trying to fit in, afraid not to agree with Fi.

"Can you believe it?" sighed Fi. "I mean, as if Superpony would look like Spike. Spike's more like the anti-Superpony. Useless-pony!"

"Oh Fi," said Jessica, uncertainly, "he's not that bad."

Fi scowled at her. "Are you disagreeing with me? Would you rather not be our friend?" she snapped. "Would you rather go riding with Hopeless Hannah and Useless-pony than with us?"

"Er... um... no... I didn't say that," stammered Jessica. "I can still ride with you, can't I?"

"I'll consider it," said Fi, smirking at Ellie. "But there's no room in our gang for traitors."

Funny, thought Hannah, because that was exactly how *she* felt about Jessica. And she also felt a little bit uncomfortable about herself, too. Hannah could see how desperately Jessica wanted to be friends with Fi and Ellie. She remembered they had talked about it often enough before they'd had ponies. They'd fantasised about how it would be, how they would all share knowledge and enjoy riding together and go to shows. The reality was nothing like the fantasy. Hannah wondered whether she was acting the same way – she had wanted to be Fi and Ellie's friend, too. But why? It wasn't working out at all well. Maybe it would get better – it was early days, yet, she decided.

"Hi Josh," said Fi, as Joshua came into the tack room for Rambo's tack. Fi twiddled a lock of her hair between her fingers as she smiled at him. "Have you read about Pony Girl and Superpony? It's all here," she added, handing Joshua the paper. Joshua stopped to read the report and look at the pictures.

"Isn't Superpony dreamy?" asked Ellie. "Don't you just wish you were a superhero, Josh?"

Joshua just grunted, handing the paper back to Fi. "At least Black Diamond has been rescued," he said, taking his tack and heading back out to the yard.

"You so fancy him," teased Fi.

"I so do *not!*" protested Ellie, turning pink.

"Liar! It's *soooooooo* obvious," Fi said, smirking. It seemed to Hannah that it was Fi who fancied Joshua. Her voice changed whenever she spoke to him – it got softer and more girly. Hannah had never heard Fi speak to Ellie,

Jessica or herself the way she spoke to Joshua. It seemed to Hannah that to Fi, Joshua already was a superhero.

"Come on, let's go riding," said Fi, and she, Ellie and Jessica got their tack, too, and left. As usual, no-one asked Hannah whether she wanted to go, but she got Spike's tack and trailed along after them, not having anyone else to ride with, and knowing they were unlikely to refuse if she was ready when they were.

Spike's plaits were still rebelling in all directions. Sighing, Hannah came to the reluctant decision that she was wasting her time. She'd take them out when she got back, she decided. Spike definitely looked better when his mane was going in all directions than he did with unruly plaits. She would just live with it, safe in the knowledge that Superpony's mane was as super as he was.

Chapter Fourteen

H ANNAH HAD ALWAYS DREAMED of taking her pony to a show. Now she had Spike, her dream was coming true.

"What classes are you entering?" Jessica asked, seeing Hannah examining the schedule for the Chipping Sanford Show and Gymkhana, due to take place at the weekend.

"Family mount, clear round jumping and… probably a couple of gymkhana games," said Hannah, running her finger down the schedule. There were classes for show ponies, jumping classes and fancy dress, as well as a ring just for gymkhana games. Fi and Ellie were bound to enter the showing and jumping, but Hannah didn't feel she and Spike were quite the showing and show jumping types. Jessica looked over her shoulder.

"I'm entering Roxy for the family mount and clear round, too," she said, "as well as the fancy dress class – my mum has made me a fantastic outfit which I'm not telling anyone about, it's a secret. Which gymkhana games will you enter?" It was like old times, thought Hannah. Jessica was being so normal, so like her old self – it was only when Fi and Ellie were around that she changed. Hannah wished she could be her old self all the time.

"Probably the mug race and the walk, trot and canter," Hannah told her friend. She didn't feel confident about any gymkhana class where she might have to get off and back on again. She couldn't quite picture Spike standing still long enough for her to remount – he didn't do it in the yard so it was unlikely he'd morph into the perfect pony at a show. She couldn't vault on, like the experienced gymkhana riders – perhaps next year she might be able to. In the meantime, she had been practising leaning over Spike's shoulder in canter to pick up a mug from a jumping block, before putting it, upside down, on a bending pole. She was actually getting quite good at it. Maybe Pony Girl was rubbing off on her, she thought.

"It's so exciting," said Jessica. "We're actually taking our own ponies to a show – remember how we used to dream about going to shows with Cloud and Major?"

"Who are Cloud and Major?" asked Fi, creeping up behind them.

"Er, just some ponies we used to... well, um... just some ponies," stammered Jessica, going pink and reverting back to being *The Traitor Jessica*.

"I've never heard of them, have you Ellie?" Fi said, as Ellie sauntered up behind her, running her finger around the inside of an empty salt-and-vinegar crisp bag to soak up the final crumbs. "They wouldn't be *imaginary* ponies, by any chance, would they?"

Jessica went from pink to bright red, shaking her head furiously.

"So what if they were?" said Hannah, ignoring the pleading look Jessica shot her. What was the big deal? "Didn't you ever have imaginary ponies before you got Florin and Strawberry Pop?" she asked.

Fi's eyebrows disappeared into her fringe in astonishment. "Of course not!" she exclaimed. "Before Florin I had a pony called Arabella, and before that I had a lead rein pony called Carisbrooke Bobbin. Ellie had a grey named Crispin. We had *real* ponies!" That she and Ellie had been so incredibly fortunate that they hadn't needed to dream up ponies didn't seem to occur to Fi.

"Come on Fi," said Ellie, pretending to gather up imaginary reins and jogging on the spot, "Cloud is impatient to go riding."

"Whoa there," cried Fi, tugging on her own imaginary reins. "I'm having trouble with Major today, he's *veeeery* fresh!" and the two of them jogged off, holding their hands in front of them as though they were riding, laughing as they disappeared into the tack room.

"What did you say that for?" asked Jessica, furious with Hannah.

"I thought they might understand," said Hannah, realising she'd made a huge mistake. How could she ever have thought Fi and Ellie would have had imaginary ponies? Now they thought even less of her – and Jessica. She'd been all kinds of stupid, again. Watching her friend run after Fi and Ellie Hannah heard herself sigh. She'd go and get Spike, he always made her feel better.

Spike was in a particularly jolly mood. Leaving his bezzie mate Moke to graze he walked bouncily beside Hannah, full of joy and anticipation. It was as though he were asking, *what fun are we going to have today?* Hannah kissed his nose and ran her fingers through his mane. She'd have to plait it again for the show, but this time she would run each plait up into a ball and sew it in close to Spike's neck. She wondered how he would look and whether she could plait his tail to match.

The day of the show dawned bright and sunny, and from very early in the morning the stable yard was full of everyone washing, plaiting and oiling hooves, getting their ponies ready for the show. Fi and Ellie plaited their ponies with experienced hands but Jessica and Hannah took far longer, with mixed results. Roxy stood with admirable patience while Jessica took her time, but Spike fidgeted at the end of his rope so Hannah had to hurry. Florin and Strawberry Pop's plaits were neat little balls of mane, evenly spaced along their necks. Roxy's plaits were much fatter, not quite even, but they still transformed her. She looked very smart. When Hannah finally finished plaiting Spike's mane, she stood back to admire her work. Maybe *admire* wasn't the right word. They were plaits all right, but they didn't all sit evenly – some stuck up a bit – and they seemed to be all different sizes. What had she done wrong? Trying to plait a moving target didn't help, of course. She wished she'd practised more.

Turning her attention to Spike's tail, she gave up after three attempts. The hair kept slipping through her fingers, the plait was all wonky and wisps kept escaping. It didn't so much neaten the tail as draw attention to the mess she'd made of it. It put Hannah in mind of a demented hedgehog. Stroking all the hair at the dock down again Hannah abandoned the idea of a plaited tail and oiled Spike's hooves. She wished – for the umpteenth time – that her pony was more like his superhero self, with defined white socks she could highlight with chalk (like Florin's snowy legs) and a beautiful amber coat which would gleam in the sunshine (like Florin's golden coat). Fi's pony looked like a fairy horse, all golden, silver and glistening in the sunlight. Even Strawberry Pop's pink dapples, and Roxy's contrasting brown-and-white patches looked wonderful. Spike just looked... well, like Spike with plaits, thought Hannah, and wonky plaits at that.

Even Joshua was going to the show. Rambo, with his hogged mane and pulled tail, took no time to prepare and soon everyone was ready. Of course, Fi and Ellie were travelling in Fi's trailer, which arrived with a flourish behind her mum's big 4X4. Florin and Strawberry Pop walked up the ramp like professionals, and Fi's mum secured the ramp behind them, motioning to Fi and Ellie to climb into the car, all their tack and riding clothes piled neatly in the back. The two girls were whisked away to the show in style just as Jessica and Hannah set off on their ponies. With no trailer they were hacking to the show, following some way back from Joshua, who rode alongside his friend Cameron on his rangy bay pony.

Sensing something was up Spike snorted with excitement, earning him annoyed looks from Jessica. Her friend looked the part, thought Hannah, noticing Jessica's brand new tweed jacket and buff jodhpurs. Her short boots were polished and she wore her black hair in two long plaits, which bounced about on her back, an emerald green ribbon at each end. Hannah was relieved she and Jessica could hack without Fi and Ellie being horrid and influencing her friend.

"Have you washed Spike's legs?" Jessica asked Hannah, with a frown. It seemed she didn't need Fi and Ellie after all. Hannah felt a frown taking over her own features – a frown of indignation. Of course she had, only it didn't seem to matter what she did to Spike's funny-coloured legs, they always looked the same. The brown of his body just seemed to sort of drain into a lighter colour. It was as though he had tie-and-dye legs – he certainly had no distinct socks like Florin. Or Superpony, Hannah thought with a sigh.

Looking at her show outfit in the mirror the previous evening, Hannah had felt quite the show rider but now she wasn't so confident. Her parents had bought her a new jacket – tweed like Jessica's – and she knew it looked good over her creamy jodhpurs and short black boots, but she felt uncomfortable in a shirt and tie (she felt as though she were at school, and she never felt good at school) and she wasn't used to riding in gloves. She had forced her mousy hair into a hairnet but already she could feel wisps escaping – just like Spike's tail had escaped all her attempts to plait it. She wished she had plaited her hair like Jessica, put it in a ponytail like Ellie, or tied it back in a net with a cheerful ribbon, like Fi.

The show was held in a huge field which resembled a bowl, sloping down from all sides onto a flat area at the centre where all the rings were roped out, and a secretary's tent, burger van and several trade stands stood to one side. Horseboxes and trailers were parked on three sides of the slopes and on the other, the flattest, was a large area where riders could ride and lunge their mounts before their classes. Among the boxes and trailers Hannah could see horses and ponies being groomed and tacked up, their riders putting the final touches to their hair and clothes, grooms holding horses so they didn't eat grass or dirty their oiled hooves. Hannah spotted Fi's mum's trailer near the ring – she'd got there early so she wasn't far from the action.

Hannah and Jessica collected their numbers from the secretary's tent and found out when their classes were due to take place. Hannah noticed how Fi and Ellie immediately replaced the shiny, white plastic tape which came with their numbers with discreet navy ribbon which matched their jackets, and Fi's mum rounded the corners of both numbers with scissors so they sat neatly on the riders' backs in lozenge shapes. Hannah didn't dare ask her to do the same for her and Jessica – Fi's mum looked well scary.

"Fi's going to look exactly like her mum when she grows up," she whispered to Jessica, who was also observing the number ritual with envy. Fi's mum was tall, poised, immaculately dressed in designer jeans and a popular brand of polo shirt, and her blonde hair was impeccably cut to frame her face. Her head was on a permanent tilt so it looked as though she had a bad smell wafting under her nose. It occurred to Hannah that Fi could have asked her mum to help them with their numbers, but such a thought obviously hadn't occurred to Fi.

Hannah thought how professional Fi and Ellie looked in all their posh show clothes. Fi wore a dark blue jacket and jodhpurs the colour of butter. Her blonde hair was fiercely contained by a hairnet and red ribbon under her blue velvet hat, and brown gloves and jodhpur boots, and a leather-covered showing cane completed her outfit. Florin's show bridle was made from thin brown leather, and below his ears sat a browband covered in red, white and blue velvet ribbon, highlighted with gold thread which glinted in the sun.

Ellie's jacket and hat were also navy but she wore putty-coloured jodhpurs and long black boots. She carried a short jumping whip and her gloves were black. She wore her chestnut hair in a long ponytail tied with a long, pink ribbon. Strawberry Pop wore overreach boots and some snowy bandages on her front legs. Both girls oozed confidence as Fi rode Florin over to the showing ring and Ellie and Strawberry Pop disappeared towards the jumping ring, leaving Jessica and Hannah feeling rather flat and unsure what to do.

"Shall we have a go at the clear round while the ponies are fresh?" suggested Hannah. Spike was quite excited, nodding his head up and down and jogging around, so Hannah thought some jumping might settle him, especially as she had already noticed a number of irritated glances in his direction from Fi and Ellie. Roxy was her usual dependable self, solid and unfazed, but it didn't seem to be rubbing off on Spike.

There were two people waiting to jump at the clear round jumping ring. Competitors just turned up, paid the entry fee and jumped. As the two riders tackled their rounds Spike managed to bounce off the collecting ring steward a couple of times and scratch his nose on one of the stakes which held the ropes. Unfortunately, one of the rings on his snaffle bit hooked itself on the stake, yanking it out so it dangled under his chin. After the steward rescued them with a frown it was their turn. Jessica and Roxy went first – and did a neat and solid clear round.

"Here you are," said the steward, handing Jessica a white *Clear Round* rosette as she trotted out of the arena.

"Well done!" cried Hannah, urging Spike into the ring and heading for the first jump, a tiny brush fence.

Jumps! Spike seemed to say, and he quickened his pace. Hannah remembered how well he'd jumped at the dealer's yard when she'd tried him (to say nothing of Superpony's amazing leap with Black Diamond), and she had practised a bit in the indoor school at Lavender Riding School so she had high hopes for a clear round. They sailed over the brush fence and Hannah steered towards jump two, an upright, which Spike took with glee. His ears were pricked, his tail swished – he really seemed to be enjoying himself and Hannah started to do the same. This was her dream, riding her own pony at a show, sailing over jumps. It was fantastic and Hannah could feel a smile on her face as they popped jump after jump, before heading towards the collecting ring again without a refusal or a pole down. Yep, Hannah was on her way to doing something right, doing something well, on the way to being Clever Hannah at last!

"What a shame," said the steward, shaking his head.

"What do you mean?" asked Hannah, looking back. All the jumps were still upright, still complete, she had jumped clear. She was due a rosette!

"Took the wrong course, love," explained the steward, motioning for her to leave the ring, the next rider already heading for the brush fence. "Why not have another go later?"

Riding past the queue of riders waiting their turn Hannah couldn't believe it – she had messed up again. Not only that, she'd let Spike down when he'd jumped so well – not that he seemed to mind, he still bobbed along under her, all bounce and enthusiasm. She felt well and truly wretched. What a start!

"Where's your rosette?" asked Jessica. Hannah looked at the snowy ribbon fluttering between Roxy's plaits. She had so wanted one – as much for Spike as for herself. When she told Jessica she'd taken the wrong course her friend didn't even look surprised, she just rolled her eyes.

Everyone expects me to mess up, Hannah thought, and they'd only be surprised if I didn't. She decided she would take the steward's advice and have another go later – but perhaps when the others were busy so if she messed up again they wouldn't know.

With time to kill before the family mount Jessica and Hannah rode over to watch Fi and Florin win their showing class. Fi rode a beautiful individual show, with Florin obeying her every command. Acting as groom in the line-up, Fi's mum removed Florin's saddle and brushed him over so that Fi could stand him up for the judge, before trotting her pony up and down. Hannah noticed the beautiful, precise markings on the palomino's quarters which Fi's mum had expertly combed on. She briefly wondered whether she could do the same on Spike's quarters, before realising it would probably be a lost cause. They'd come out all wonky, she decided, and make Spike look wonky, too.

They congratulated Fi as she rode out after a lap of honour and Fi actually smiled. Hannah thought hard. Yes, she decided, that was the first real smile she'd see on Fi's face, rather than the usual smirk. They were joined by Ellie and Strawberry Pop, who also sported a red rosette from their jumping class. Everyone had a rosette, thought Hannah. Except for her and Spike. Nobody remarked on it, or seemed to think it odd or even a shame. Never mind, thought Hannah, she and Spike still had time to shine in the family mount class.

Then she spotted her parents by the ringside, waving to her.

Chapter Fifteen

"THERE YOU ARE!" SAID her mum, giving Spike a mint. "Have you been in any classes yet?"

"Of course she hasn't, she hasn't got any rosettes!" said her dad, smiling at his daughter. Hannah felt the heavy weight of expectation on her shoulders. Results – in the form of rosettes – were what they had come for.

"Hello Mrs and Mrs Pearson," said Jessica, bringing Roxy to a halt next to Spike.

"Oh, hello Jessica – what have you won?" asked Hannah's mum, peering at Roxy's rosette.

"It's just a clear round rosette," explained Jessica, modestly, even though her chest swelled with obvious pride.

"Why don't you go in for that?" Hannah's dad asked Hannah.

Hannah's heart sank. "I did," she said.

"Where's your rosette then, darling?" asked her mum, as though Hannah only had to enter and a clear round – with its reward of a rosette – was hers.

"We didn't get a clear round," explained Hannah, biting her lip. She caught her dad doing the eye-rolling thing, just as Jessica had done. Clearly she wasn't living up to his expectation that having a pony would turn his daughter into a person who was good at something – for a change.

"Why you didn't have that dappled grey pony or that yellowy one over there, I'll never know," Hannah's dad muttered, ignoring murderous looks hurled in his direction from Hannah's mum. "That is the pony – one of them – you turned down, isn't it?" he added, screwing up his eyes and looking at Florin.

"It wasn't Spike's fault," cried Hannah, patting her pony's neck. "I took the wrong course. Spike jumped perfectly."

Her confession didn't seem to improve her father's mood. Spike jiggled about in a jolly way, bouncing off a car and narrowly missing treading on her mother's toes. They all trooped across the showground towards where the family pony class was due to start, passing Fi and Ellie on the way.

"Are these your friends?" asked Hannah's mum, as Jessica started talking with them. "Hello, we're Hannah's parents."

Fi and Ellie managed to look even more superior – something Hannah wouldn't have thought possible. Fi's mum smiled without warmth.

"Hannah could have had your pony," her father said, nodding at Florin, "but she chose this fellow here, instead, from the dealer. Still don't know why," he added in a confidential tone to Fi's mum.

Fi's mum's neck shot back into her collar in astonishment. Fi blinked several times and Hannah heard a loud snigger escape from Ellie.

"You're mistaken, Mr… er…" Fi's mum began, in a voice even farther back than usual. "Fiona has had Florin for several years – we bought him from a top showing family in the Cotswolds. He certainly has never passed through the hands of a…a *dealer*." She said the word *dealer* as though the sound of it broke shards of glass in her mouth.

"Dad, that's not the same pony!" hissed Hannah, wishing she could just disappear through the ground.

"Really?" asked her father, surprised. "Well I never, it looks exactly the same."

Wishing her parents hadn't turned up to watch her, Hannah rode over to the collecting ring with Jessica for the family mount class. Jessica's parents were also there and they chatted, far more successfully, with Hannah's, having shared bench seats in Lavender Riding School's gallery when Jessica and Hannah had been taking lessons on riding school ponies. Looking around her, Hannah could see that the family mount class had attracted a large number of entries. *A horse or pony suitable to be ridden by any member of the family* the show schedule stated. There were heavyweight cobs, hunter types and stocky ponies like Roxy, in all shapes, colours and sizes. Hannah decided she would hate to be the judge – what a difficult class to decide!

The steward, a woman in a tweed skirt and a corduroy jacket, beckoned them all into the ring and everyone rode around, close to the ropes. The judge, a large woman in a floaty, flowery dress and a straw hat, stood in the middle with her chin between her thumb and forefinger, obviously lost in thought. Spike wanted to jog when everyone walked. When everyone trotted he cantered sideways, pulling the reins out of Hannah's hands. He seemed very excited and thrilled to be at the party. The pony in front of Hannah, a skinny grey ridden by an equally skinny girl, kept looking back nervously and then, suddenly, the skinny girl began to cry.

"Circle away!" commanded the tweed-and-corduroy ring steward, waving her clipboard at Hannah as she passed. Hannah didn't know what she meant so she just kept going, hoping the steward wouldn't notice. Everyone changed the rein and went around in the opposite direction and Hannah steered Spike around to join them. Again they walked, trotted and cantered and Spike did exactly that – he just didn't do it at the same time as everyone else. Hannah's heart sank.

"Spike," she implored, tugging at the reins, "please be good, please just do what everyone else is doing." The worst part was that Spike seemed to really be enjoying himself – he wasn't being nasty and he wasn't upset. He was just excited and happy.

As the steward asked everyone to walk the skinny girl steered her grey pony into a corner and dismounted, wailing at the steward and pointing at Hannah. And then something rather wonderful happened, something Hannah had dreamed of, waited for, longed for, had always harboured hope of: the judge beckoned to Hannah to come to the centre of the ring. Hannah could hardly believe it – was she really being called in first, to head the line-up in the family mount?

No.

She wasn't.

"I'm afraid I'm going to have to ask you to leave the ring, you're upsetting some of the other competitors," explained the judge, kindly but firmly. I think your pony needs more experience before he enters a show again, don't you?"

How is he going to get more experience, thought Hannah, if I have to leave the ring? Crestfallen, she headed Spike for the collecting ring, aware that everyone was staring at her, relieved that she – the disruptive influence – was leaving.

"What's going on?" asked her dad, confused.

"Didn't you want to stay, darling?" asked her mother.

Hannah explained. "He's just a bit excited, that's all, it doesn't matter," she said, patting Spike's neck loyally, aware that her father was less than pleased and her mother, too, was disappointed. They had bought her a pony to see their daughter shine and it wasn't working out at all as anyone had planned. If only she could tell them about Spike being Superpony, thought Hannah. But of course, she couldn't. She doubted they'd believe her, even if she did – and who could blame them?

Hannah didn't think she could ever feel as wretched as she did right at that moment. She'd been sent out of the ring at a show, in front of everyone.

"I ought to give that judge a piece of my mind," Hannah's father cried, rolling up his sleeves and lifting the ring rope. "Who does she think she is, asking you to leave the ring? You've paid your entry fee like everybody else…"

I was wrong, thought Hannah. I feel more wretched now at the prospect of my dad threatening to make a scene.

"Please don't Dad," she implored. "You'll only make things worse. Pleeeeese!"

"Hannah's right, Derek," said her mum, "it won't make any difference."

"Oh all right," said her father, crossly. "We might as well head off home then, there's a match on this afternoon I'd like to watch."

Loosely translated, thought Hannah, as *Hannah's not going to win anything so we might as well stop wasting our time here.*

"Enjoy the rest of your day, darling," said her mother, before scuttling off after her father.

Hannah felt the familiar feeling of having let people down – of letting herself down. "Oh Spike," she said, stroking his neck which was now hot and damp with sweat, "we have to be good at something, don't we? If only we can find out what it is!"

Unwilling to watch the outcome of the family pony class (Jessica and Roxy had been pulled in fourth, she noticed), Hannah headed Spike over to the gymkhana ring where Joshua and Rambo were busy beating other competitors in heats, qualifying for finals and winning rosettes. Without a mane on which to hang the rosettes, two blue, one red and a yellow fluttered from the number tape around Joshua's waist. He hadn't bothered to change the white tape for anything fancy, Hannah noticed.

Hoping Spike's exuberance would be a help in the gymkhana games Hannah lined up for the walk, trot and canter. It was a simple race – walk one length of the ring, turn and trot the next and finish with a length at canter. Surely she and Spike could manage that? It turned out they could, but Spike broke pace several times, meaning they had to turn a circle each time and lose valuable seconds, which cost them a place in the final – which was won by Joshua and Rambo, earning them another red ribbon.

"There's only the mug race left," Hannah said wistfully, lining up between a long-legged girl on a bay pony and a freckled boy on a dun. As the whistle blew Hannah headed Spike down the field and picked up the first mug, asking Spike to turn back so she could place it, upside down, on the first bending pole – which she did. Soon there were only two more mugs to go. With one securely on the pole Hannah headed Spike back for the last, leaning over and grabbing it securely. All her hard work was paying off she thought, incredulously. With the last bending pole in sight, and the long-legged girl and freckled boy behind her, Hannah knew she was in with a shout – until she dropped her mug. Spike trod on it, squashing it flat. The freckled boy overtook her with a whoop and Hannah rode Spike out of the ring, having failed to qualify for the final.

"Well that's that, Spike," said Hannah, rubbing her pony's ears. "That's our last class. We could have another go at the clear round if you like – perhaps in a little while when you've cooled down – and I'll try not to let you down again."

Spike nuzzled Hannah and blew snot on her jodhpurs. *It doesn't matter*, he seemed to say. *It's only a show, they're only ribbons, it's not important.*

Hannah knew he was right but she couldn't help thinking it wasn't just the show, not just the rosettes. She felt disappointed that her dreams were still just dreams. She'd had such high hopes about getting a pony – she had dreamed of being good at something. How could it still be going so wrong?

Chapter Sixteen

A T THE RINGSIDE, HANNAH manoeuvred Spike between a family having a picnic and a pile of jumps in order to watch the fancy dress class. Pulling the reins out of her hands Spike started to graze and Hannah didn't have the heart to stop him. One of his plaits had come undone and was unravelling in the middle of his neck. She'd have to get off and sort it out. She looked in the ring for Jessica – her friend had made such a big thing about her fancy dress she couldn't wait to see it. As she stood up in her stirrups Spike cropped grass closer and closer to the family and their picnic. Suddenly, one of the children screamed and the mother snatched her up into her arms.

"What do you think you're doing?" she shouted at Hannah, whose attention was sharply distracted from the ring. "Your pony has eaten my Charlene's sandwich!"

"Oh Spike!" cried Hannah, hastily gathering up her reins and thinking fast. "What sort of sandwich was it?"

"What does that matter?" screamed the mother, thoroughly unreasonably Hannah thought. She tried to explain.

"Well, if it were cheese, that would be okay," she began, "but if it were ham, for example, or chicken, well that's quite dangerous for a pony to eat..."

"It was egg mayonnaise, for your information!" snorted the woman. "But the point you seem to be missing is that your pony could have *bitten* Charlene. He's dangerous!"

"Oh, well, did he?" asked Hannah, her heart sinking into her boots. She couldn't imagine Spike biting anyone. The woman examined Charlene's hand – all fingers were present and correct and no blood appeared to be pumping from an injury.

"No, she seems to be all right," the woman told her – Hannah thought she sounded quite disappointed. "But all the same, you should take your pony somewhere else. He's dangerous!"

Sighing, Hannah headed Spike away from the ring. She could still see the entries for the fancy dress from further away – there were a great many of them, even more than in the family mount which had earned Roxy a green rosette for fourth place. The fancy dress class was popular with tiny children who could hardly ride, hoping the judge would be swayed by their cuteness, as well as older riders with quite sophisticated outfits. Hannah could see three fairies, two Ninja Turtles, a couple of robots, a character from a popular children's television programme and no fewer than… Hannah could hardly believe it, she actually did a double-take like a cartoon character… *six Pony Girls* and *Superponies*, all done up in costumes like the ones she and Spike wore on their adventures, some good, some – well, it had to be said – downright awful.

"Well," exclaimed Hannah, recognising one of them – a good one – as her friend Jessica and Roxy. "Can you believe it Spike! What do you make of that?"

Spike couldn't care less. In fact, he was suddenly very interested in something going on at the top of the hill in front of them. He stood, his hooves planted, his neck stretched, his head high, staring towards the other side of the show ring, perfectly still for once – for which Hannah was grateful as it meant she could relax for a moment. But then she grew suspicious – it was so very un-Spike-like for him to be so still. Following his gaze, Hannah couldn't make out what was so enthralling. And then, as though snapped out of a spell, Spike spun around, carrying Hannah past all the spectators at the ringside, past the secretary's tent and the burger van, past Fi's mum's car and trailer where Fi and Ellie were sitting on canvas chairs and trying not to spill anything down their riding clothes as they munched dainty sandwiches, and on towards where the majority of horseboxes were parked. They were cantering by the time they reached the row of temporary toilets, and as soon as they were behind the blue plastic pods and out of sight Hannah realised, with complete certainty, what was about to happen.

Sure enough Spike leapt into the air, there was the now familiar ZAPPING and POWING sounds, the whooshing before the red, amber and green lights flashed before her eyes, and Hannah felt herself turn inside out then outside in. When they landed she was once again wearing her Pony Girl outfit, complete with cape and mask, and Spike was the wonderful Superpony with his amazing mane and tail, and his brilliant-white legs.

Hannah had no idea why they were needed there, at the show. Everything in the horsebox park seemed normal – unless there were horse thieves at work, Hannah thought. Perhaps someone was stealing a horsebox, or tack, or a pony or child were in danger. Why were she and Superpony there? What were they there to do? Who were they there to rescue?

And then she saw the problem – and what a problem it was, Hannah thought with a gasp of horror. One of the horseboxes, a huge, shiny horsebox with living accommodation and room for several horses, was rumbling its way down the hill. That wouldn't have been a worry had it not been for one thing: as they raced towards it Hannah could plainly see that the cab was empty – except for a very worried looking Jack Russell jumping up and down at the window, barking. With no-one at the steering wheel the horsebox trundled down the hill towards the showground, picking up speed with every second, completely out of control and with no chance of it stopping!

"Come on Spike!" cried Hannah, urging her pony on towards the runaway horsebox. "We have to stop it somehow." Spike needed no encouragement, and sweeping around in a semi-circle they were soon racing up behind the horsebox, Spike galloping as fast as he could, Hannah's cape streaming out behind them like a banner.

"Faster Spike, faster Superpony!" urged Hannah, praying there were no horses or ponies inside the horsebox. If there were, the situation was as grim for them as it was for everyone in the horsebox's path. She could see the showground laid out below them. Everyone was so caught up with the excitement of the fancy dress class no-one had spotted the catastrophe about to happen. If Pony Girl and Superpony couldn't stop the horsebox it would plough down the hillside and into the show ring, and who knew what carnage would be the result!

Leaning forward, Hannah implored her pony for greater effort even though she knew he was going as fast as he could. She could hear the pounding of his hooves on the grass, hear the terrified barking of the Jack Russell in the cab getting louder and louder as her gallant pony galloped his heart out to catch up with the runaway horsebox. They were gaining on it – but their progress seemed so very slow. But then, suddenly, they were almost alongside and Hannah felt she could lean over and touch the rear ramp. On they galloped, Superpony getting faster as they passed the rear wheels, gradually gaining on the cab. And then, miraculously, they were level with it and without hesitation Pony Girl leant over to wrestle open the door, praying it wasn't locked. Superpony galloped straight and true, never faltering as his rider stood up in her stirrups and grasped the door handle. It was time for Hannah to take over, she had to get into the cab! Hauling herself up she leapt towards it, her feet on the saddle in order to push herself up and on to the side of the horsebox cab. And then, somehow, the door was open and she was inside with the Jack Russell which was now whimpering with fear, its ears and tail down, its eyes showing terror.

Already, the horsebox had reached the show field. Through the windscreen Pony Girl saw people running away, heard mothers screaming, snatching up their offspring and shouting to others. Horses and ponies were rearing, riders were falling, and all the while the horsebox hurtled on towards the ring where tiny tots on ponies were being led about.

One of these is the brake, Hannah thought, forcing her eyes away from the nightmare scene before her to look down through the steering wheel to three pedals. She didn't know how to drive but she knew one of the pedals would be the right one. It was just a case of choosing it. Filled with a confidence which was new to her, and with the unfamiliar feeling of trust in her own judgement, Hannah grasped the steering wheel and gingerly pushed her foot down onto the centre pedal. The horsebox faltered, it slowed. It was the right pedal! Aware of the sea of horses and ponies parting before her, of people running out of the horsebox's path, Hannah pushed down again, harder, with all the weight she could muster, and the horsebox juddered as the force and weight of it struggled against the brakes. The Jack Russell was thrown forward onto the windscreen and Hannah heard an indignant yelp as it bounced off it and onto the floor of the cab. Hannah pushed her foot down again, as hard as she could, steering towards a break in the cars parked around the ringside, the horsebox swaying dangerously, threatening to overturn as it ploughed on. It juddered again, slowed right down, and came to a creaking stop centimetres from the ropes.

Hannah felt drained and elated at the same time. She had done it – she and Superpony had done it! The Jack Russell started barking again in a, 'I knew it would be okay really', sort of manner and licked Hannah's face in grateful thanks. People surrounded the cab, the doors were flung open and the owner of the horsebox grasped the Jack Russell and gushed her thanks. Pony Girl was carried aloft by grateful showgoers, all elated at being saved by their superhero.

"Where's Sp…Superpony?" asked Hannah in her Pony Girl voice, and spotted him being led towards her. Reunited, Hannah patted her pony's neck. "You were wonderful, you're the best pony ever," she whispered, mounting him once more. Turning, Pony Girl waved to the cheering crowd.

'Thanks Pony Girl! Hurrah for Superpony! Three cheers for the Superheroes!' the crowd cried, and Hannah spotted Fi, Ellie and Jessica in among the throng, cheering just as enthusiastically. They don't know it's me, Hannah thought.

Pushing their way to the front, Fi asked shyly whether she could have a selfie, and Pony Girl and Superpony obliged. Of course this had a snowball effect and it was some time before Pony Girl and Superpony could get away from all the selfies and handshakes and pats on the back. Everyone wanted to talk to them or stroke Superpony's famous golden mane – including, Hannah saw with some amusement – the family which had accused her of having a dangerous pony and had shooed her away. Now they wanted nothing more than to pat that same pony's nose and take a picture with the girl who couldn't control him, excited at having something they could share on social media and boast about to their friends. Hannah even signed autographs, including several on people's t-shirts. How funny, thought Hannah, wondering what they would all say if they knew the truth about the identities of the superheroes.

Suddenly, Superpony grew restless and Pony Girl sensed it was time to put an end to all the PR. Waving to the crowd she turned Superpony around and they rode away despite cries of, 'Don't go, Pony Girl,' and 'Stay a bit longer, Superpony!' After some ZAPPING and POWING and flashing colours behind the temporary toilets they were back to their old selves.

"Did you see them?" Jessica asked Hannah breathlessly when she and Spike caught up with them. Everything had settled down and the fancy dress class had finally been judged. Hannah nodded.

"Weren't they amazing? They saved the day by stopping that horsebox, the owners were so very grateful. And look, don't you think I look just like her, and Roxy looks like Superpony? What do you think of our outfits?"

Hannah agreed that they were, indeed, splendid, and very similar to the real thing – even though she could see that Jessica's mum had made Jessica's cape out of the curtains which used to be in Jessica's bedroom, and that Roxy's auburn mane and tail were made from wool.

"Did you win?" she asked her.

"No, some tiny child in a shop-bought fairy costume came first, just because the judge thought she looked adorable. And she cried," said Jessica, bitterly.

"Why did the judge cry?" asked Hannah.

"No, you nitwit, the child cried, not the judge!" exclaimed Jessica.

Well, thought Hannah, one moment I'm Pony Girl and adored by one and all, the next moment I'm a nitwit.

Back at the yard, Fi, Ellie and Jessica all talked non-stop about the show, rosettes won and lost, Superpony and how they all wanted to be just like Pony Girl.

"Imagine having a pony like Superpony!" said Fi. "I mean, Florin's great, but Superpony's so, well, *sooooooooooooo*, *you* know."

"Yes," agreed Ellie, "he's just so, well, *super!*"

"Did you get a selfie with Pony Girl?" Jessica asked.

"Yes!" chorused Fi and Ellie. "Didn't you?"

No-one seemed to notice (or care) that Hannah wasn't joining in. Hannah was lost in her own thoughts. She remembered how she had felt leaping from Superpony's saddle into the horsebox cab, the thrill of knowing she was the only one who could stop the runaway horsebox, the certainty she had felt when she had selected the right pedal to stop its journey and how confident she had been, so sure of herself. This time, she remembered, she had known what to do and had done it. On their previous encounters, Superpony had been the one making all the decisions and she'd just been along for the ride. When she was Pony Girl, Hannah realised with a jolt, she was exactly the person she'd always dreamed of being.

Hannah realised she never had gone back for a second go at the clear round jumping. Somehow, it didn't seem to matter any more that she hadn't won any rosettes. Spike was right, she thought, as she undid all his unruly plaits and ran her fingers through his curly mane, rosettes really didn't matter at all.

Chapter Seventeen

"Have you seen what Joshua has taped up inside his locker?" giggled Ellie, two weeks after the Chipping Sanford show.

Fi turned around and gave her a stare. "What?" she asked, suddenly interested.

"A *picture* of someone…" Ellie began, teasingly.

"Who?" asked Jessica, joining in. "Is it someone we know?"

"Oh yes," Ellie replied, looking at Fi, who seemed to be smirking. "It's obviously someone Joshua likes. A lot. In fact, it must be someone he would like to get to know better."

Hannah couldn't help overhearing. Since the show and her rescue of the horsebox she had spent more and more time by herself, rather than hang around with Jessica who had, in turn, hung around with Fi and Ellie. She just didn't feel the need to be looked down upon – even if Fi and Ellie were much better riders than she, and their ponies were capable of winning classes at shows. Thinking very hard about it, Hannah was certain she wasn't jealous of them (as she had been before she had Spike). It was more that she preferred spending time with her own pony. He was better company and much more fun, and when she was with him she felt much better about herself instead of feeling inferior. Hannah was fed up with that feeling, and since her Pony Girl adventure with the horsebox she had made up her mind not to hang out with anyone who was negative about her, if she could possibly help it. Why should she? After all, wasn't she Pony Girl, and wasn't Spike Superpony? Knowing that made Hannah realise that Fi and Ellie didn't know everything, and she could imagine how silly they would feel if they ever found out. Unfortunately, Spike was stabled in the livery yard so it was impossible to avoid them all completely – which was how she heard Ellie's revelation about Joshua's secret pin-up.

Hannah could see Fi's eyes shining and it suddenly dawned on her that Fi believed Joshua had *her* picture in his locker. She wondered whether it could be true. She couldn't see Joshua and Fi together somehow, but who knew how boys' minds worked? And Fi was pretty, there was no denying it.

"Come on, he's there now so we'll be able to see it if you're quick!" said Ellie, already heading for the tack room. Fi sprinted after her and Jessica grabbed Hannah's arm and pulled her along too, even though Hannah wasn't very interested. Sure enough, Joshua was rummaging around in his locker, pulling out bits of tack and trying to identify them. By the state of them, they had been in his locker for some time.

"Hi Josh!" said Ellie, smiling. Joshua mumbled something back without looking up. Walking over to the locker, Ellie pulled the door wide. "What are you doing?" she asked.

As the locker door swung open the subject of Joshua's affections was revealed – and it wasn't Fi. Instead, two cuttings from the local newspaper and a close-up of Pony Girl on Superpony were sticky-taped to the inside of the door.

Fi managed to look disappointed and murderous at the same time, which was some doing. For once, Hannah was glad nobody took any notice of her for she was certain her face was turning pinker than Strawberry Pop's tail.

"In love with Pony Girl are you?" teased Ellie, fully aware of how annoyed Fi was.

Joshua said nothing, just wrestled the locker door from Ellie's grasp and slammed it shut with a bang.

"Josh and Pony Girl!" chanted Ellie, childishly, "Pony Girl and Josh!"

"Haven't you got something more productive to do?" asked Joshua, determined not to lose his cool – which was tricky as he too was turning crimson.

"Fiona's very upset – she thought you liked *her*," Ellie went on. Suddenly, Hannah realised that Ellie liked Joshua just as much as Fi did, and was relieved to discover her friend wasn't Joshua's favoured pin-up, as Fi always suggested.

"Shut up, Ellie, you're *sooooo* making a fool of yourself," said Fi, regaining her composure. Hannah hoped she'd regained her own. Whatever would Joshua say if he realised that Pony Girl was standing right behind him? Except that she wasn't Pony Girl, at least not all the time, and particularly not now. And, Hannah decided, there was no way he would ever discover Pony Girl's real identity – not from Pony Girl herself, anyway. She now had a double reason for not revealing her secret. How embarrassing would it be for both of them if Joshua realised the true identity of his pin-up? Hannah felt her stomach flip at the mere thought. This Pony Girl thing had more far-reaching consequences than she had realised. It was mind blowing!

Hannah went to her own locker and collected her grooming kit, her thoughts in turmoil. Tying Spike up outside his stable she got to work brushing his patchy chestnut coat, trying to coax its dullness into shining, and making yet another attempt to get her pony's mane to lie flat. She concentrated doubly hard so she had no room in her head to think about Joshua's locker and the pictures pinned up inside the door.

Spike nuzzled her arm and she planted a kiss on his nose, her mind working overtime, her heart suddenly full. How wonderful her pony was, she thought, realising just how much he meant to her. He was her friend – the best friend she could have wished for. How lucky she was to have him. She remembered the negative feelings she'd had about him when he'd first arrived, and scolded herself for caring about what other people thought – wrongly she realised – about her pony. He was just perfect, Spike was.

Hannah mused about how her opinions of the other ponies had changed over the last few months. How could she have been jealous of Fi, Ellie and Jessica and their ponies? How could she ever have considered Spike inferior to any of them?

Hannah's thoughts turned to Florin. Florin was very tidy in his stable – he never dug up his bed, or rolled, or spilt his water. He always chewed his hay thoughtfully and politely. Spike was almost thug-like by comparison – Spike was the anti-Florin. But then, Hannah remembered, Florin never nuzzled Fi or frisked her for sweets. Florin was far too polite and well mannered and, Hannah was beginning to think, a teensy-weensy bit... well, *predictable*. And possibly a bit, well, dare she say, *dull?* He was a lovely pony, he was beautiful and he won rosettes but Hannah could no longer imagine the palomino pony belonging to her. She had once, but not any more.

And come to think of it, Hannah realised, unable and unwilling to stop her rambling thoughts, Strawberry Pop wasn't very friendly, either. She was quite highly strung and Ellie couldn't have much fun on her. She had trouble with Pop getting all excited on hacks, she had a thing about dogs and often shied at nothing. She was certainly no fun pony but she was – and no-one could argue the fact – an amazing jumping machine.

Roxy was a nice pony, but not friendly and enthusiastic like Spike, thought Hannah. Whereas Spike was fun, Roxy wasn't. She just did as she was asked, the perfect first pony.

No, Hannah decided, looking at the ponies in a new light, she wouldn't swap any of them for her Spike, even – and she realised this with a jolt – even if Spike *never turned into Superpony again!* Spike was fun. Spike was her friend. In fact, Spike was everybody's friend, if they weren't too stuck-up to be his. And he was no snob, either. Take Moke: none of the other ponies had ever hung out with him and he must have been lonely before Spike turned up and made him his chum. How *nice* Spike was. In fact, Hannah thought, far from being a pony to be despised or made fun of, as Fi and Ellie obviously thought, Spike was a shining example!

"I'm going to try to be more like you, Spike," Hannah told her pony as she brushed his mane. It still went in all different directions but Hannah decided she *liked* it. How *boring* it would be to have a pony with a tame mane, she decided. How very *ordinary*.

"I no longer want to be Clever Hannah or Hannah who wins rosettes," she whispered to Spike, "I want to be Spike's friend Hannah. Because actually Spike, you're not only Superpony, but you're a pretty *super pony*, too."

Hannah's super pony leant his head on her shoulder so she could feel the warmth of him through her t-shirt. Without knowing why, Hannah felt a lump in her throat. He was her pony and she was his person. They were a real partnership and Hannah knew that if she made no other friends at the stables, she no longer cared. Spike was the one, true friend she needed and she was so, so lucky to have him. She'd been right to choose him at the dealer's yard. They had picked each other for the team – team Spike and Hannah!

Saddling up, Hannah thought she might go in the school and try Spike over some jumps. If she ever wanted to succeed in clear round jumping, she thought, she would have to learn how to remember a course. As soon as she was in the saddle, however, Jessica appeared and Hannah was amazed when she asked whether she might ride out with her.

"Er, okay, but aren't you riding with Fi and Ellie?" she asked.

"Um, I was, but they're going somewhere else," her friend mumbled, hurrying to saddle Roxy, who looked pained at being rushed.

Surprised, Hannah turned Spike to walk in step with Roxy, and the pair left the yard and headed out to the bridle path, Jessica sniffing. Hannah waited until they reached the woods before asking what was wrong.

"Nothing," said Jessica, rather too quickly. Then, when Hannah didn't pursue it, it all came out in a rush.

"Oh, everything's wrong," Jessica cried. "Fi said I hold her and Ellie back whenever we go riding, and Ellie said it was difficult riding in a threesome and a pair was better. When I said you could come too and we could ride in two pairs they said it still wouldn't work, especially with Spike because he upset the other ponies. They obviously just don't want me to ride with them. I thought they were my friends!"

Thinking back to her earlier thoughts about Fi, Ellie and their ponies, Hannah decided she wasn't upset about not being welcome out riding with Princess Fi and Princess Ellie, as Joshua called them, especially as they were so rude about Spike. But she could see it still mattered to Jessica. She wondered whether she should suggest to her that Fi and Ellie had never been Jessica's real friends, but decided it might be a bit too much for Jessica to hear right now.

"Well," she said, "we can always ride out together – you and me. After all," she continued, "we've got our own ponies now. We don't have to always trail along in Fi and Ellie's wake."

"But they know so much more than us," said Jessica, looking shocked. "I mean, they're Fi and Ellie, remember how we dreamed of being their friends?"

Hannah shrugged. "Well, things change," she said. "You have to admit that they're not exactly friendly, are they?"

Jessica gulped and said nothing. For once, Hannah noticed, Spike was walking like a normal pony, quietly, without jogging and jiggling and being all bouncy. In fact, he and Roxy were walking in step, enjoying each other's company. It made a peaceful change from Fi having to always ride in front, and Ellie squeaking at them not to crowd her. It was, Hannah thought with a jolt, exactly the sort of ride she and Jessica had always talked about and dreamed of before they'd got their own ponies.

"Roxy likes Spike," said Jessica, suddenly. Hannah knew she never would have said such a thing in front of Fi or Ellie.

"He's a nice pony," said Hannah, patting his neck. "Actually," she corrected herself, "he's a *super* pony!" Spike nodded his head up and down as though agreeing with her and Hannah laughed.

They rode on, cantering on the open parts of the bridle path, walking along the narrow parts, enjoying their ponies and riding together. It was a lovely sunny day and several walkers were striding along enjoying the outdoors. Hannah and Jessica had to pull up from a canter at one spot so as not to scare walkers with their dogs, before continuing side-by-side.

They were heading toward a busy spot where the footpath and bridle path ran adjacent to each other, and the bridle path stretched out ahead of them, a fence on either side, the path narrowing before it branched off into two separate tracks further along. Suddenly the peace was shattered by the sound of galloping hoof beats and loud screams, and Hannah and Jessica turned to see a pony in the distance galloping up behind them, the rider out of control.

"It's Strawberry Pop!" gasped Jessica, soothing Roxy who was snorting nervously.

Ellie sat in the saddle, hauling on the reins. Hannah could see that Strawberry Pop was beyond listening to her rider and the reason was plain to see – a large dog bounded behind the pony, snapping at its heels, excited by the chase. In a second when the scene before her seemed to freeze Hannah could see the whites of Strawberry Pop's terrified eyes, hear the barking of the dog and, in the distance behind them, caught sight of Fi on Florin, and the dog's owner, chasing in vain.

"What can we do?" asked Jessica. But Hannah was looking ahead to the track where Strawberry Pop would have to go, along the narrow bridle path in front of them, and she caught sight of something that made her catch her breath, her heart leaping into her mouth. A tiny child had ducked adventurously under the fence and was wandering along the bridle path, his mother some distance away and oblivious to the danger approaching.

It was a terrible, terrible situation, which could only end badly.

Unless....

Instinctively and without hesitation Hannah knew what Pony Girl and Superpony had to do. Urging Spike forward she headed him towards the child. Spike, picking up on her urgency, launched willingly into a gallop. But Strawberry Pop was in full flight, already up to speed and thundering along behind them. She would be upon them at any moment – could Superpony outrun her in time?

With the sound of Spike's hoof beats joining Strawberry Pop's Hannah leant forward, remembering the times she had practised leaning down to grasp a mug for the mug race. This was the most important race of her life – and that of the child's ahead of her. She could hear the sound of galloping hoof beats behind her, hear the snapping of the dog's jaws as it gave chase to its quarry, heard sobs and screams from Ellie, still trying to stop her terrified pony. Hannah leant down the side of her pony's chestnut neck as they were almost upon the toddler seeing, out of the corner of her eye and on the other side of the fence, the child's now hysterical mother, too far away to help.

Whoosh! Spike swept past the child and Hannah grasped the back of his jacket like a mug's handle, hauling him upwards out of danger and galloping on to the next fork in the path as Strawberry Pop stormed up behind them, the mother's screams ringing in her ears. At the fork Spike turned right and Hannah watched, relieved, as Ellie and Strawberry Pop flew past her to the left, the dog tiring and disappearing through the trees back to its owner, leaving the pony to gallop on alone.

Hannah now had another problem – the child. Amazingly, the little boy was laughing, having thoroughly enjoyed his adventure.

"Horsy!" he gurgled, burying his fingers in Spike's wayward mane. Putting the boy astride her pony's withers, Hannah turned back along the bridle path to the sobbing mother who grabbed her child, gabbled a thank you, and held the boy so closely they seemed to morph into a single being.

"You might like to walk some way away from the bridleway in future," Hannah suggested, before walking back to Jessica and Fi who had caught up with her. They both stared open-mouthed at Hannah as she reined in Spike, dismounted and threw her arms around his neck, telling him how wonderful he was.

"Wow Hannah," whispered Jessica, her eyes like saucers.

"You…" said Fi, in a quivering voice, "… you were just like Pony Girl or something. What… I mean… how on earth did you *do* that?"

Hannah gulped. Pony Girl – well, yes, that was right, she was Pony Girl!

Except that…

She looked at Spike. Yes, the same old Spike, patchy chestnut in colour, bonkers mane, wishy-washy legs. She glanced down at her own clothes: pink jodhpurs, lemon t-shirt.

No cape.

No mask.

No Lycra suit.

Hannah gulped. When she had urged Spike forward she felt as though she were Pony Girl, riding Superpony – but she was just Hannah, and he was just Spike. How could she have done something so right when she was Hannah? It seemed that she hadn't needed the metamorphosis, the POW, the whooshing sound, the traffic lights. Could it really be true that she, *Hannah*, had known what needed to be done and had done it? Throughout the whole rescue it had seemed to her as though she *had* been Pony Girl. Where did Hannah end and Pony Girl begin? Who was the true heroine?

"We'd better find Ellie," she said, her mind racing. Unwilling to let her new-found confidence desert her Hannah remounted and headed Spike on after Strawberry Pop's hoof prints, leaving Fi and Jessica to trail after her, open mouthed in amazed silence.

"Can you believe what just happened?" whispered Jessica.

Fi slowly shook her head and gulped. "I would *neeeeeever* have been able to do what Hannah just did," she said, without even realising just what a totally un-Fi-like thing she had just uttered.

They found Ellie further on, dismounted, weeping, holding a wide-eyed and sweating Strawberry Pop by her reins. Jumping off Spike, Hannah quickly looked over

Strawberry Pop – thankfully, the pony had no bites or injuries.

"She was terrified," sniffed Ellie, wiping tears away with her sleeve as fast as new ones fell onto her cheeks. "And so was I," she added. "I think the dog could sense Strawberry Pop's fear, and that just encouraged it to chase her."

"Do you think you can ride home?" asked Hannah, taking the lead in the absence of any input from Fi and Jessica, who were still in shock.

Ellie shook her head fiercely, too shaken to get back on. "I don't want to. I'll lead Pop home," she said.

"But home is miles away," said Hannah. "Why don't you ride Spike? I don't mind riding Pop." The words were out of her mouth before she realised. What was she saying? Ellie would never let Hannah ride her precious pony. She waited for her to sneer, to tell her she wasn't good enough to ride Strawberry Pop, waited for her to turn up her nose at Spike, her – as Ellie saw it – second-rate pony. But Hannah was wrong. Ellie couldn't wait to hand her pony over and she scrambled up onto Spike who, instead of shaking his head and marching off as usual, stood like a rock, sympathetic to Ellie's fears. Hannah noticed Ellie giving her chestnut pony a grateful pat and she mounted Pop, sitting as quietly as she could to give the pony confidence.

The four of them set off for home, walking in stunned silence. Strawberry Pop jogged and snatched at the reins, still upset, but Hannah was used to Spike's jogging and she sat still, allowing the pony to calm down. It wasn't until they were almost back at the yard, and Ellie had begun talking almost normally again, that Hannah realised she had been in the lead all the time, Fi, for once, having forfeited her usual place. Far from having the nut-do Fi always said he would, Florin seemed perfectly happy tucked in behind Spike, level with Roxy – a development not lost on Hannah, who was keeping Pop walking on a long rein to relax her. The pony was still nervous but by the time they reached Lavender Riding School she had dried off and Ellie was almost back to her old self. Riding into the yard, however, caused some raised eyebrows.

"Whatever are you doing on Ellie's pony?" asked Joshua, looking from Hannah to Ellie in amazement.

"Long story," said Hannah, dismounting.

"Hannah is a *heroine*," announced Jessica, unable to keep the drama from her voice.

Hannah cringed, waiting for the protests from Fi and Ellie. But none came.

"She was just like Pony Girl," Ellie said, tears welling up in her eyes again as she remembered her horrible experience.

"She really was," agreed Fi. "Hannah was amazing, just *ahhh-maaa-zing*."

Hannah almost fell over.

"And so was Spike," said Ellie, hugging his patchy chestnut neck before swapping ponies with Hannah, who by now believed she was in a dream and would wake up at any moment. Rescuing the child from being trampled she could believe (she was getting used to adventures), but hearing Fi and Ellie sing the praises of herself and her pony was much harder to take in.

"It was all Spike," said Hannah, giving him the credit and a hug. "He's the best pony in the world."

"Yes," sniffed Ellie, "I think he probably is."

Something had shifted, thought Hannah, things had changed. Something in the way Fi and Ellie spoke to her, talked to Joshua about her, was different.

She didn't think it would last.

Chapter Eighteen

Had it been up to Hannah nobody would have known about the daring rescue she and Spike had performed on the bridle path. But because Fi and Ellie and Jessica were all involved, and Hannah had been Hannah and not Pony Girl, and Joshua had seen her astride Strawberry Pop there was no getting away from it. Soon, everyone at the yard knew about the amazing adventure.

"Our real-life Pony Girl!" Jessica kept saying, which made Hannah cringe, even though she knew nobody would ever link her with the real Pony Girl. Least of all Joshua, she thought. She *hoped*.

"It was all Spike, honestly," Hannah said, wishing everyone would stop talking about it. But they didn't – at least not for a week or so, and then things gradually went back to normal.

Only things weren't quite as they had been before. Hannah was right, something had shifted – and not just with Fi and Ellie. Something had changed inside herself. Feeling more confident and less impressed by Fi and Ellie, Hannah stopped trying to hang out with them. And so did Jessica, who started to hang around with Hannah instead. Hannah and Jessica became friends again – just like old times. And just as they stopped wanting to be friends with Fi and Ellie a strange thing happened: Fi and Ellie suddenly wanted to be friends with Hannah and Jessica and stopped being so superior and sneery. Fi still occasionally stuck her nose in the air like she had a smell under it, and Ellie hated anyone crowding Strawberry Pop on hacks and panicked a bit whenever a dog was about (which was understandable), but generally the four of them began to get on pretty well.

Ellie even helped Hannah with her jumping. Spike loved it – and was almost as good at it as Strawberry Pop (only with added head shaking and excited snorting), and Hannah occasionally remembered the jumping courses, which meant they won some rosettes. But that wasn't important to Hannah any more. What was important was her relationship with Spike.

And everyone else's relationship with Spike changed, too. Fi and Ellie stopped saying horrible things about him; Jessica started to be nice to him. Instead of laughing at him and his funny ways everyone started to appreciate Spike and the way he loved life. Even Joshua seemed to be friendlier to everyone. He was particularly friendly with Hannah – probably because she was the only girl on the yard who didn't go all silly whenever he was around, and she could have a proper conversation with him without twiddling her hair or batting her eyelashes, which he appreciated. Joshua found it very annoying when the other girls did it. It was, he thought, like talking to someone who had had their brain removed.

Some things didn't change. Hannah didn't suddenly become brilliant at everything; she was still pretty rubbish at most of her school work and she still dreaded PE – but now she didn't really mind. Because now she had Spike, and she had friends and she was comfortable with herself. In short, she realised she had nothing to prove. She was good at something after all. Everyone is – only sometimes it can take a long time to find out what that something is. Getting a pony – the right pony – had certainly had the desired effect, even though it had happened in a roundabout, unpredictable way she could never have foreseen.

An absence of disasters at Lavender Riding School and the surrounding area meant that since the daring horsebox rescue at the Chipping Sanford Show the services of Pony Girl and Superpony hadn't been needed, but Hannah was confident that she and Spike could once again be anywhere they needed to be. Hannah even had a sneaking suspicion in the back of her mind that team Hannah and Spike might be able to cope with a mini disaster by themselves – after all, they had done it before!

Chapter Nineteen

I T WAS A VERY hot summer's day at school when Hannah, having been picked last (again) for the rounders team, awaited her turn to bat. As she stood in line, the warmth of the sun on her shoulders, Hannah's mind drifted – as it often did – back to her Pony Girl adventures. As the school playing field seemed to disappear around her she imagined herself on Spike, remembered the occasions when she had been Pony Girl, recalled the great feeling she had experienced, the feeling of knowing exactly what to do and when to do it. Hearing someone shout her name Hannah's eyes focused once again on her surroundings, only to see the ball hurtling towards her like an off-course planet. Still with her head firmly in Pony Girl mode, and with no time to think, Hannah swung the bat to meet it.

The ball didn't sail past the bat.

It didn't fly upwards before landing in the backstop's hands.

Nobody called *out!*

Instead, Hannah heard a *crack* as the bat met the ball and she watched, open-mouthed (as did everyone else), as it soared off over everyone's heads to the very edge of the sports field, just exactly as she had always imagined it might do.

It really did.

The ball bounced off the perimeter fence and Hannah ran an easy rounder – mainly because everyone on the pitch was rooted to the ground in shock. Did Hannah actually manage to score the winning rounder for the first time in her life? Nobody can remember because as Hannah stormed past first base Miss Craig, observing the miracle in front of her that was Hannah's bat connecting with the ball gulped, and then inhaled when she should have exhaled, swallowing her whistle. Clutching at her throat and gasping like a fish out of water, she gained the attention of everyone around her. Her gain was Hannah's loss.

Luckily, tall and lanky Sam Marner who, with a future career as a doctor in mind never missed an after-school first aid session, wasn't about to let an opportunity to put his training into practice slip by. Grabbing the astonished (and blueing) Miss Craig from behind and around her ribcage, Sam wasted no time performing an abdominal thrust, designed to bring up what should never have gone down. Upon the reappearance of the whistle and the recovery of Miss Craig he was, quite rightly, hailed as hero of the hour, snatching any glory Hannah had been due.

Which just proved, thought Hannah, that even when your moment of success finally arrives it can still be overshadowed by something even more unexpected, and nothing whatsoever to do with you. And although she acknowledged that saving Miss Craig's life was far, *far* more important than running a rounder, Hannah couldn't help feeling that the way things had worked out was pretty typical of her luck!

It wasn't until much later that week, after she'd been struggling with long jump (again), that Hannah wondered what she might achieve if she imagined herself as Pony Girl whenever she found herself in a challenging situation (which happened quite a lot of the time). After all, she asked herself, what was the worst that could happen, providing Miss Craig (or anyone else) didn't have a whistle in her mouth? Hannah decided she would look out for that and pick her moment to experiment.

Whispering her plan to Spike that evening she was sure she saw a glint in his eye which signalled approval. Or, Hannah decided, it could just have been her pony's way of reminding her to fetch the carrots.

So she did.

 Matador